HAUNTED

By Shaun

C000061999

Books by the Author

To my family for their belief and support. To Lottie for always being willing to talk through the story with me. To Sarah and Al for once again keeping me on the straight and narrow. And, to everyone that believes in ghosts and the supernatural, even if only for a little while.

Chapter 1

The bank of shiny, black, unblinking eyes, untouched by the light in which Jane worked, stared down from the gloom. Careful to stay in the blind spot above and behind Jane, the spider inched forward. It froze whenever Jane moved and flattened its dark body against the ceiling. It was used to this. This was what evolution had shaped it to do. It was a hunter. A killer without mercy or remorse and it made steady, patient progress until directly over Jane's head. Once there, it settled in to wait.

Jane was oblivious to the creature. She was absorbed by the images on her monitor and clicked on one after the other, stopping every now and then to make notes on a large, well-used notepad.

'Spiders in the United Kingdom that have a bite that can pierce human skin:

The Woodlouse Spider—Dysdera Crocata;

The Tube Web Spider—Segestria Florentina;

The Cardinal Spider—Tegenaria Parietina.'

She used her notepad to create maps of where they could be found in the country and carefully wrote down information such as: what their habitat was like, how they trapped their prey, and most importantly, how they could be killed. The Latin names of the creatures made no sense, but she was a diligent student and noted them down

1

anyway, her brimming notepad testament to the hours of work she had put in researching her subject.

A gentle knock at the door caused her to hurriedly minimise the screen and bring up her emails.

"Hello," she replied to the knock. Her mother opened the bedroom door as Jane placed a magazine on top of the notepad, hoping to hide what she had been writing.

"It's late Jane." Her mother caught Jane straightening the magazine so that it covered the notepad. "Please tell me you're not looking at spiders again."

"I've just had a quick look mum, I've been doing homework... mostly."

"Mostly... come on Jane it's time to leave all that behind. We've talked about this." Her mother launched into another monologue. "It's your future that's important. I know it's difficult for you, but you need to look forward. You're bright and you're so beautiful, but you're wasting away stuck in here staring at spiders on the internet." Jane's mother repeated the words that she had said many times before, over the preceding months, and Jane had heard many times. But it was hard to move on, too hard. "What would Jack say sweetheart?"

"I know mum... I know. And I will... leave it behind, I mean. Don't worry," Jane clicked 'Shut Down' and stood up. "I'll go to bed," she said and blew her mum a kiss. "Goodnight," she continued and tried to throw some extra cheer into her tone, but it didn't really work.

"Night love." Her mother's voice was edged in concern. She looked like she might say something more—but didn't—she had said it all before.

Jane waited until her mother had closed the door, before starting her walkabout. First, she checked the window was latched. Then she surveyed the back garden, looking for anything out of the ordinary, before pulling down the blackout blinds, unfurling the mosquito net that had been rolled up for the daytime, and drawing the curtains tightly closed. Once the curtains were in place, she carefully pressed the Velcro that lined the edges of the curtains against the Velcro glued to the wall, until the curtains were firmly sealed, and no gaps remained. A quick squirt of fly spray, along the edges of the curtain, finished the defensive line. Satisfied with the window, Jane picked up a butterfly net that had been leaning idly against the wall and began her patrol around the room.

The room was bare. In the aftermath of the events in January, Jane had removed all her posters from her room and painted her walls white. She had made her parents remove the carpets that had provided her bare feet with comfort, then painted the floorboards white. She had removed all clutter from her previously very messy room and packed it up, or thrown it away.

Now as she stalked around, looking over every inch of the bare room, she was confident that anything that flew, walked, crawled, scuttled or slid would be easily visible against the white background.

She spotted the black spider, motionless on the ceiling.

Jane was reminded, as she always was when she saw a spider, to earlier that year, to her encounter with the giant spiders that had captured Jack and chased Ginny and her through the graveyard. The encounter was still fresh in her mind, bright and vivid like blood on white blotting-paper. Not faded in the slightest by the six months that had passed. Jane remembered the way the spiders had sunk their fangs into their prey—*no not prey—her friends!* And then cocooned them in web and suspended them from the ceiling to be eaten later.

The experience had traumatised Jane and left her determined to be better prepared, just in case they returned. She recalled the powerlessness she had felt and her frustration at being so weak. Well never again, she thought, next time I'll be ready for them.

"Got you," she positioned the net under the spider and gave it a quick spray with the aerosol. The spider dropped into the net, spasmed and died.

Jane watched gleefully, savouring every moment. She enjoyed the power of life and death she had over the spider, especially the death part.

"Who's your daddy?" she mocked. The fire of revenge burned inside her and gave her strength. Spiders were now her least favourite creature and she would kill as many of them as she could, rather than let one of them harm her, or her friends, ever again.

She dropped the motionless body into her waste bin and shut the lid—just in case the spider returned to life. Then she took a deep breath and looked at her bed. It used to be one of her favourite places. She loved to sleep and always slept in late at the weekend, but not anymore. Nowadays, she avoided sleep until exhaustion took her and she had no choice but to lay in her bed's choking claustrophobic embrace. Every night, the bedcovers weighed her down, pinning her in her nightmares, as she wrestled them for every fitful moment of sleep. Until dawn broke, allowing daylight to rescue her. Then she would rise from her sweat-soaked twisted sheets—unrested, unrestored and traumatised.

The bed was the epicentre of Jane's terrors. Her ground zero. So she circled it warily, before pulling the cover back and climbing in. She lay there with the lights still on and her eyes open, determined to fight off sleep for as long as she could. It was at least an hour, before her mind slowed and her eyelids closed in defeat.

Chapter 2

Death came to Ginny every night, when her thoughts slipped from conscious to unconscious and sleep narrowed the distance between the living and the dead. Death took advantage, waited for her to sleep, then bridged the reduced gap between realms and haunted Ginny's dreams.

Every night, she found herself in her recurring nightmare that had so often painted the nights of her life in black horror. A dark mass chased her through streets and across fields. It was an absence of light that moved steadily, passing through and over anything in its path, leaving all life spoiled and dying in its wake. She could feel the mass behind her. It licked at her back with cold tendrils, as she ran. Its silence was as profound as its absence of light. It was the nothingness of death. The absence of life. It was what came afterwards, when your last breath leaked from your body. It was oblivion.

Before January, she used to awaken before the dark mass caught her, with her sweat soaked bedsheets sticking to her. But everything had changed in January, when she had died and been taken by Death. She recalled the blackness, the nothingness of her death, the timelessness of it. She could have been dead for a thousand years because time stopped when she was dead and there only nothing—just nothing—and there would have always been just nothing, forever. The reality, though, was that she was only dead for minutes. Then she returned. She was alive again and now every night her legs would not run fast enough and every night the dark mass enveloped her, and every night it killed her in her sleep.

Night after night, she was killed, again and again, surrounded by the cold darkness. She sucked in the dark, deep into her lungs, and drowned in death. It suffocated her. It poisoned her. It bled her dry and crushed her. There was no escape. And then once she was dead, Death spoke in her mind in her own voice; her inner voice that should have been hers, and hers alone. Death violated it with words that did not belong there; words that told her what she must do to end the nightmares.

Death reminded her that she had willingly given herself to Death in the graveyard in the snow and yet she lived again. And that Alfred, the shame of Middle Gratestone, had willingly given himself to Death in the graveyard, one-hundred-years before her, and yet he also lived again. He reminded her that Alfred Thatcher, the youngest and longest lived of the Thatcher brothers, had died and been taken by Death in the graveyard in the snow. And he told her that that made two living and one dead.

The balance was wrong. It should be two living and two dead. Someone still needed to die.

Death told Ginny this every night, after he killed her in her dreams.

Chapter 3

Jane woke quickly, opened her eyes and rolled out from under her white bedcover in one fluid movement. She scanned the room, before retrieving the butterfly net and fly spray and then started patrolling the walls. Once she was certain that the room was clear, she switched on the computer and brought up the feed from her motion cameras. She had bought them off the internet and rigged them up around the house to cover the back gate, back path, front and backdoor, and the front garden. They were infrared, motion-sensitive cameras that snapped a picture of anything passing by. They were meant to be used for catching photos of wildlife, which was just what she needed them for. She browsed through the pictures of a badger and morning birds caught in the lens, then, once she was sure there was nothing else, opened her emails.

"Good, the meet is still on," she said to herself.

Jane wasn't sure if anything remotely satisfactory would come out of the meeting, but it was better than doing nothing. She had done too much of doing nothing, for too long. She felt like the spiders had cocooned her in her house, as surely as they had cocooned Jack and Ginny back in January. She was trapped here, just like her friends had been in the web. It was just too exhausting to go outside. Jane took a deep breath.

"I will win," she said. "I will win," stronger this time. "I will win." Another deep breath. "Please let me win." Jane looked herself in the eye in the mirror on her white dressing table. It was the only item there. It stood on its own and waited for Jane to fill its glass face every morning. For Jane, it was a portal to her inner-self and only when she stared into it did she let her mask slip and allow the bruised, battered young girl to look out. She did that now. The eyes that stared back were still as green as ever, but their brightness was gone. Her face was devoid of make-up because her cosmetics had been a casualty of the clear out and her hair was cut short to prevent any spiders crawling in and hiding there. Jane sighed, nothing good ever came of looking in the mirror.

What does Jack see in me? She questioned herself. He's tall, clever, handsome and funny. He's everything, but I'm a wreck.

"It's just a matter of time until he dumps me," she grumbled to herself, as she wrenched her gaze away from the hard truth that she saw in the mirror.

She dressed in jeans and a long-sleeve top then packed her bag, filling it with bug bombs, fly spray, insect repellent, pepper spray, a rape alarm and other sundry weapons useful against spiders, insects and people. It was bulky and dug into her hip when she slung it over her shoulder, but these days she didn't go anywhere without her trusty bag.

The closer she got to being ready to go out, the more her mind and body started to resist her attempts to get dressed as if trying to protect her from the dangers of the outside world. She pulled her boots on, they felt like lead.

She picked up her pack, it was full of lead. She took another deep breath then stood up.

The door to her bedroom caught her eye. The door to the outside.

"Okay," she encouraged herself and walked to the door. With one hand holding a can of fly spray she placed the other hand on the door handle, twisted and pulled the door open. A faint waft of bacon found her nose, so she breathed in the aroma.

Not fresh, she thought, but then her mum and dad should be out by now. Perhaps, they had left some, she hoped. She pulled the door closed behind her then surveyed the corridor. Tempting as it was, to rush down and look for cooked bacon, she forced herself to look up and down the upstairs landing. It was not as white and sterile out here as in her room, so Jane concentrated, scanning methodically around the walls, ceiling and carpet. She tracked her eye line with the fly spray, and only once she was certain that the landing was clear, did she move away from the safety of her room and head downstairs. She walked slowly, scanning as she went; it paid to be careful. Sure enough, in the hall, a housefly buzzed around the hallway light, turning at impossibly sharp angles to avoid flying into the walls. Jane stepped forward and blasted it out of the air with the fly spray, then cast around for more before entering and clearing the kitchen in the same manner.

After a delicious breakfast of cold bacon on freshly baked bread, Jane felt a little strength and confidence return and she was ready to face the outside world and the creatures it contained.

She left the house, making sure all the doors were shut behind her to stop any bugs getting in while she was out, and headed for Church Road, following the route she normally took to school. Today it was Saturday, so the commuters that busied around on weekdays were elsewhere. Jane tried to appreciate the scenery as she walked and raise the interest that she used to have in everything that she saw.

She had been a bright outgoing girl once. People had flocked to her and she had shone with life, but now the same people scorned her. She was the weird girl now. *The spider girl!* The girl people talked about behind her back. Nobody wanted to be her friend.

Jane stopped as she crossed the old bridge that led onto Church Road, to watch the pond skaters running across the top of the water, bending the surface as they passed without breaking through and sinking into the cold depths below. The stream was crystal clear and if it wasn't for the dimples made by the pond skaters' feet, they would have seemed to walk on air. Below them, fish hovered over the riverbed while green weeds swayed in the lazy current.

Life should have been good for Jane, but she was tired from lack of sleep and worried about what the dreams meant. With a sigh, she crossed the bridge and walked along the path that ran alongside the church. The trees that lined the road were heavily foliaged with thick leaves, greened by the spring sun and thickened by the fresh water drawn up by their deep roots. The shade they provided was cool and dark. Up ahead, near the church gate, a figure separated from the shadow of a thick gnarled trunk and stepped into the path.

"Hey Jane."

"Hi Jack," a warm smile crossed Jane's face, but she couldn't hold it in place. "Is it just us?"

"Yes, I think so. The others will be along soon, or maybe they're already there. I haven't checked the church yet."

They looked at each other for a moment then hugged. Jane pulled away first and brushed at her hair, trying to do something to make its shortness pretty. She was conscious that her lack of hair and lack of makeup made her look unattractive and she worried endlessly that Jack would leave her. The alternative however, of allowing something to crawl in and hide in her hair was worse. She looked at Jack. Her handsome Jack. And felt safer. He had grown taller and broader in the six months they had been together and Jane loved everything about him.

If only I wasn't so ugly, she thought.

"You look beautiful," Jack said. Perhaps it was because she brushed at her hair, but Jack always seemed to know what she was thinking. His blue eyes searched hers and his brow wrinkled in concentration.

"Stop being gallant," Jane replied.

But Jack meant it. Her eyes seemed bigger now; they were always wide open in fear or apprehension and always on the lookout, but that let the light into them so that they sparkled. Her short hair let Jack see her graceful swan-neck and uncovered the arch of her back. Her skin devoid of makeup, was clear of all blemishes and glowed in the sun, but somehow also remained mysterious in the shade. Every day when Jack saw Jane he thought the same thing—that he had never seen her look so beautiful. He took her face in his hands and kissed her gently on the lips.

"Carry your bag?" he offered without drawing back.

"No, you know I can't do without it. I never know when something in there might come in handy," Jane blushed and felt better.

"I had the dream again," Jack said and straightened to his full height. Their conversations always started like this. Other people started with: 'Lovely weather,' 'how's your mum?' or 'what did you do last night?' With Jack and Jane, it was always: 'I had the dream again.'

"Yeah me too," Jane replied with the confirmation Jack expected. "It was totally the same as before."

"Yeah, I got killed too," said Jack. "Just once it would be nice to get away."

"Do you think they'll ever stop?"

"Death is telling us to rebalance things Jane. I don't think it will stop until one of us is dead."

13

"Why does it have to be one of us though? Why not someone else?" asked Jane.

"I don't know," replied Jack. "Come on, let's go," he abruptly changed the subject.

They started to amble at a snail's pace along the path, Jane's shoulder occasionally brushing Jack's upper arm. They looked like they didn't want to get to where they were heading. The graveyard wall passed slowly alongside them.

"We have to assume that it has to be one of the four of us that are having the dream that is supposed to die. You..." Jack shuddered, "me, Ginny or Dave."

"Yes, that's all of us that were there. But what if we don't die? Will we just carry on having the dreams or will something worse happen?" Jane asked.

"I don't know Jane. I wish I did."

"I don't think that's even the worst of it either," Jane said quietly—secretively.

"What do you mean?" Jack raised his eyebrows.

"Well now I know that ghosts are real, and people return from being dead, and there's an angel of death and there's monsters... well now I think of other things as well."

"Like what?"

"Heaven and hell, God and the Devil, angels and demons...maybe they all exist. Maybe everything in the bible, and in legends and books... maybe they're all real. Maybe they're not just made-up stories. Every time I see a show on TV now, or read something, I start wondering if it's real. Maybe the person that wrote the script didn't make

14

it up at all, but they saw it somewhere. Vampires, werewolves, everything... everything could be real."

"I know what you mean," said Jack. "I was thinking about life and death, and what happened to us—it's impossible not to really—anyway I came here to the church when no one else was here and picked up a bible. I started flicking through it, and then started to really read it—you know. I understood it and believed it. I concentrated on the meaning of the words and what caused them to be written down. And like you I thought... maybe it's not all made-up... maybe it's all real. But that's good."

"Good! How is that good?"

"Because that means there is a god and there is a heaven and miracles can happen... and that's really amazing."

"Well I just see monsters."

Chapter 4

Alfred sat on a straw bale inside a ramshackle barn. He was shaded from the sun and out of sight of his tormentors.

"It's not meant to be like this," he said to the dusty floor, knowing it wouldn't reply, but needing to voice his thoughts anyway.

A light wind, funnelled by the valley in which the barn stood, blew through the barndoor, cooling the sweat on his brow that had been put there by too much work in the heat of late spring. He looked down at his hands, they were scabbed on the knuckles and calloused on the palms.

He had expected his new life to be like his old life; the one he had before his parents died that was happy and full of love. But it just hadn't turned out like that. "I want my life back," he lamented. He thought back to earlier that year: to back in the graveyard, when Death had gifted him a new life. He had hoped that happiness and contentment would follow. But they hadn't.

An urgent movement caught his eye, interrupting his thoughts. He looked at the barn wall next to the open door; a web hung there and shimmered as the spider that stood guard in it, silently tapped out a warning. Alfred jumped to his feet, grabbed the broom he had leant against the straw bale, and set to work once again on the dusty floor.

Joe Tanner walked in and eyed Alfred suspiciously.

"Not slacking, are you? There's plenty more for you to do after this if you want feeding tonight."

"No, not slacking." Alfred didn't look at his foster father—if you could call him that. He had learnt in the poorhouse that the best way to avoid a beating was to look down and use as few words as possible in reply. He wasn't afraid though. He had previously been dead for one-hundred-years. He was not so easy to frighten after that. But a beating was a beating nonetheless and best avoided. Fat Joe, as Alfred referred to his foster father in the secrecy of his own head, had already used the cow whip on him once today.

"Good. Don't forget what happened this morning," Fat Joe said, referring to the cow whip he had used on Alfred's back earlier. Alfred had a raised, red stripe there—he wouldn't forget in a hurry.

Fat Joe sipped tea from his 'No1 Dad' mug while watching Alfred sweep the dust and broken-up straw towards the barndoor.

"The Council is coming tomorrow to check on you. So, you can have a bath," he said. "Mildred will put the good clothes on your bed tonight for you to wear tomorrow."

"Thank you," Alfred replied. Not because he meant it but to stop Fat Joe getting angry. It had been two weeks since he'd been allowed a proper bath and that didn't warrant thanking anyone.

Alfred's dust pile reached Fat Joe, so Alfred stopped brushing and stood still for a moment, waiting, then looked

17

up. 'No1 Dad' held so close in front of Fat Joe's ruddy, sunburnt face was too much of a contradiction. Those words just did not belong to him. He had cheeks that were as taut and swollen as ripe tomatoes, hair that was mousy and lank, and eyes that were too close together, more pig-like than human.

Alfred vowed to smash the mug at the first opportunity.

Fat Joe remained where he was, eyeing Alfred, as if waiting for Alfred's disguise of obedience to slip and uncover the dissent behind. The disguise remained in place though, as impenetrable as a lead-lined wall, so Fat Joe turned and left the barn without another word. Alfred waited for the footsteps to recede and then looked at the spider in the web.

"Thank you," he said, and meant it this time.

Chapter 5

Jack and Jane quietened as they passed between Alfred Thatcher's cottage on the one side of the road and Alfred's cracked open statue on the other. The cottage had a faded 'For Sale' sign, planted in the centre of the wildly overgrown front garden and was being sold for a fraction of its worth, and yet, despite intensive cleaning, there was still an odour inside that put off all potential buyers. The dead bodies that had hung upside down in the kitchen for so long, putrefying and leaking over the floor, had left an indelible legacy.

Jane looked at Alfred's statue and thought about him. No one had seen him since the night he had come back from the dead. Jane presumed he must be alive somewhere because of the dreams she was having, but he had disappeared from Middle Gratestone and entered the anonymous state welfare system. She had no idea where he was now. The statue didn't scare her anymore though. The malevolence it once exuded was gone and now it was just an old broken piece of rock.

They reached the gate and entered the church grounds. The grass was freshly mown and flowers were dotted about, gifted by relatives of the people buried there. As Jack and Jane moved deeper into the graveyard, the gravestones became older and the flowers fewer as the living relatives that remembered those who had died, grew fewer in number and ultimately passed away themselves, leaving

19

graves unkempt and unloved. The oldest gravestones were only decorated with weeds—time forgetting everyone in the end.

"There they are," Jack spotted two pairs of legs sticking out from behind a statue. One pair sturdy and dressed in jeans and trainers, the other, slender and brown, tipped in white ankle socks and tennis shoes. The two pairs of legs were not side by side. Ginny and Dave had not worked through all their issues and it was very unlikely that Ginny would ever fully forgive Dave for being willing to sacrifice her to save his dad, but now she at least tried to be civil to him.

Jack rounded the statue first. "Hey guys," he announced their arrival.

"Hi Jack... Jane," Ginny replied as Jane also rounded the statue. Dave got to his feet slowly and stuck a hand out to Jack.

"Alright mate," they greeted each other without smiling. Jack had also not forgotten that Dave had been willing to sacrifice him as well, but he appreciated that Dave had been protecting Jane.

They were an unlikely bunch. There was a lot of distrust between them and if it wasn't necessary, they would never have met like this by personal choice. They all settled on the grass, except Jane who placed a picnic blanket down first, gave it a generous squirt of fly-spray, then sat down to form the last side of a square.

"I can't take it anymore," Dave started. "The dream is getting more and more real. I'm starting to smell the grass when I'm running through the fields and then rotten flesh when Death catches me and cold when he kills me. It's too real and it's getting more real. I'm scared that one night I just won't wake up afterwards." Dave twisted his hands, causing his biceps and pecs to juggle under his T-shirt in demonstration of the six-months hard training at the gym that he had used to dull the fear that churned inside him. His eyes flicked between the other three and the graveyard in constant surveillance. His face lean from worry, on top of training, on top of worry.

Jane nodded. "My angel of death kills me with her sword. I felt it go through me last night, then she ripped me with her vulture claws. I felt the claws digging into me and heard my flesh tearing apart," she shuddered. "If it gets anymore real, I'll either go mad or actually be dead."

Dave and Jane looked at Ginny. She was the only other one of them to talk about her dream. Jack admitted to having the dream and being killed in it but never actually spoke about the details. He just looked down at the ground and avoided catching anyone's eye.

"I felt like I was drowning in Death last night," Ginny took her turn. "The mist caught me as usual and smothered me... then filled my lungs with rotten stench that choked me. It was horrendous. Then I woke up. But yeah, it's more and more real every night... but the message at the end was the same as usual, 'the balance is wrong, it should be two living and two dead, someone still needs to die.'"

Jane glanced at Jack, but he was looking down. "So, what do we do?" she directed the question at the top of his head then looked at both Dave and Ginny to include them.

"I think it's obvious what we have to do," said Dave. "But before we get to that I think we all need to agree to speak openly and honestly. No secrets and no lies, and don't get upset if someone says something you don't want to hear." He looked at each of them to ensure they knew he meant it.

"You too Dave," said Ginny. "You're going to hear things that you don't want to hear. So, you too."

"Yeah, me too. We all need to agree."

"Agreed," they all chimed in one after the other.

"So, since it's so obvious Dave, why don't you enlighten us?" Ginny challenged.

Dave paused before answering, as if gathering his courage. He looked serious and a little worried. He glanced at Ginny, trying to anticipate her reaction, then determinedly pushed on. "Well, my interpretation of the dream is that one too many people were brought back from the dead. That means someone needs to go back to being dead to balance things out..." Dave trailed off, looking at Ginny.

"Thought so," said Ginny. "Your interpretation is that someone who was dead should go back to being dead. Well that's me and Alfred, and Alfred isn't here." Ginny leapt to her feet. "Come on then Dave let's see if you've got the guts." She stood over Dave on her tanned and toned long legs, like an Amazonian warrior princess—blonde hair sailing out behind her, and arms rigid in readiness for battle.

"No," shouted Jane and jumped up as well. Jack and Dave remained seated, neither one wanting to escalate the situation quite so soon. Jane tried to calm Ginny. "No secrets, no lies, and don't get upset. That's what we agreed. Dave's said his piece, now it's someone else's turn."

"No offence meant," Dave said, looking at Ginny as if she was already dead.

Ginny noted the look and sat back down, a little further back than last time. "So, we look for Alfred then," said Ginny.

"Look where? I've been looking on the internet for ages," Jane replied. "Jack's dad doesn't know where he is, so how do we find him?" She sat back down, content she had prevented a confrontation, but nobody answered. Dave continued to stare at Ginny, who glared defiantly back.

Dave broke the silence. "Well if I were to play the devil's advocate... I've said what I wanted to say, but I'm not necessarily correct. After all, I die in my dream, Jane dies in hers and you die in yours Ginny. So, perhaps any one of us could rebalance things. Death hasn't specified which one of us it should be."

"But you still think it's me," stated Ginny.

"On balance, I think so yes, but I'm not certain. And I don't know how to be certain... without actually killing you of course."

"Come on guys. Are we actually talking about killing someone here? Listen to yourselves, it's crazy. None of us would ever do that. No way, never." Jane shook her head vehemently.

"Kill yourself then," said Dave.

Jack looked up and tensed. They all saw it—saw the look in Jack's eye, and the intent in his body position. Dave quickly defended himself.

"Relax Jack. No secrets, no lies, remember. But without Alfred, who is it going to be?"

"So, would you kill Alfred if he was here then Dave? A thirteen-year-old boy?" asked Jane.

"A thirteen-year-old boy who should be dead, remember!" Dave started to raise his voice but then caught himself and swallowed his frustration. "Sorry—a boy who should be dead. It's not natural that he is alive at all. That is how we should restore the balance, but perhaps that is not what Death wants. After all, he brought Alfred back from the dead... so maybe it's Alfred that he wants to live and one of us that he wants to die... and on reflection, I think it's probably Ginny."

"No," said Jane. "Not Ginny. Ginny died because she was the bravest of us. She took Jack's place and my place," Jane looked directly at Ginny. "I will not repay you Ginny, by having you die for me again. No way. It's not fair."

Ginny smiled gratefully at Jane.

"Volunteer then Jane," Dave jumped in, seeing an opportunity.

"You volunteer Dave. Do the decent thing for once— nobody likes you anyway," Ginny defended Jane and launched her hatred of Dave at him.

"Maybe I'll volunteer to kill you Ginny, or at least start with you!" Dave retorted. His anger was unchecked now. He flushed red at the neck and his face tightened, making him grimace and turning his lips into a sneer. He started to get up, his eyes full of menace. Jane glanced into them and saw the unguarded hurt and anger within. Dave was acting on instinct and not with any measure of control. She leapt to her feet, getting there before Dave got to his and placed her hands, palms inward, on the sides of his face.

"Dave," she soothed softly, her face right in front of his as she looked into his angry, scared eyes. "Dave..." even softer.

Dave relaxed and sat back with a sigh. Jane continued to hold him but turned and looked between Jack and Ginny.

"Nobody is killing anybody. Or themselves. There must be another solution... and until we find another solution, we will not do anything stupid." Jane held Dave's face a moment longer then moved away and sat back down on her blanket.

They were all quiet now. Jane could hear pigeons cooing in the trees dotted around in the graveyard and bees that buzzed through looking for sweet nectar. Life was going on around them as normal while they talked about death. Jane used the lull in conversation to look around at the other three.

Who could she trust? Ginny had saved her once before, but perhaps that debt was paid now. Jack was too quiet. He was hiding something and despite their love it unsettled Jane. Dave was too angry. He might lash out and do some permanent damage to any of them. "I don't think we're getting anywhere," she timidly dipped her toe into the silence. "We're not murderers. We can't go around trying to kill each other. How about we just try to get through one night at a time. We can talk again tomorrow. Maybe something will be different in the dreams... maybe we'll get a clue what to do," she finished hopefully.

Jack looked up and let his eyes take in all of Jane. Her dark hair was cut short and allowed him a clear, wonderous view of her face. Her eyes sparkled as they flashed around looking at them all and her short hair waved across her sun-touched cheeks as she turned left and right. Her lips were parted, and she was slightly breathless from talking quickly. Jack took in the detail of her cheekbones and the tiny tip of ear that poked through her hair and he committed it all to memory. Jane's face burned into his mind and stayed there to be remembered forever. Because Jack knew what had to be done. Death had already given him the clue.

It wasn't Death that tracked down and killed him in his dreams. It was Jane. She slew him night after night with a huge scythe. It had a bone handle, fashioned from human thigh bones fused together and engraved with runes. The blade was black except for the long, curved cutting edge that shined like a crescent moon in a dark winter night sky. Its blade was ever cold against Jack's neck and he felt its icy edge every night before it cut clean through.

Jane not Death, was his killer. Night after night, she slew him and slowly turned him against her. She was his torturer and as much as he loved her, and tried to stay true, she warped his mind so that now all he wanted was to end the madness of his dreams.

"Yes, let's wait for a clue," he said with a hoarse voice. "Then we'll know what to do," although he already knew what to do.

"Yeah, okay," Jane was surprised that Jack had agreed so quickly. But even more surprised by the monotone way in which the agreement was delivered.

"Alright we can talk in the 'chat room' in the morning... if we wake up of course... to see what's new," conceded Dave, clearly disgruntled by the turn in proceedings. He eyed Ginny as if deciding whether to kill her there and then.

"See you all later," Ginny slammed the door on the discussion and walked off without looking back.

"I'm going to stay for a bit. You can all shove off," Dave spoke to their backs as they all walked away.

Chapter 6

Alfred walked through the gloom of the barn, skirting the beams of light that came from holes in the roof. The beams formed bright columns in the otherwise dingy interior and patterned the dusty floor in patches of gold.

Chains and animal harnesses hung on the back wall at head height, looking like torture instruments stored in a dungeon. Below them, blunted, rusty tools, leant lop-sided against the wall. They were dirtied the same colour as the earth on which they had once laboured. The barn smelt of the musty haybales that were stacked in the hayloft and along the side walls. The air was cool and damp in the gloom.

After a quick glance over his shoulder, Alfred pushed at the backdoor, squeaked it open then closed it gently behind him and walked away from the barn. Fat Joe had checked up on him now, so he wouldn't be back for an hour. That gave Alfred some free time.

His mood lifted as he walked away towards the outer perimeter of the farm. He heard skylarks singing as they hovered high up in the clear air and crows that cawed as they pecked around in the fields. Cows lowing in the distance added to the farmland noises. The sun and the breeze warmed and cooled him in equal measure, and he breathed in the fresh country air.

It was good to breathe again. It was good to be alive again. But someone still had to pay for what had been done to him.

He thought about his past. One-hundred-years ago, his parents and brother had been robbed and killed by the murderous townsfolk of Middle Gratestone then he had been robbed and killed by the same thieves and murderers. But Death hadn't delivered him to the afterlife. Instead, Alfred remained in limbo, trapped in a statue in the graveyard—neither dead nor alive—until Death could fulfil a promise made and resurrect him. After being trapped in the statue for one-hundred-years, he and his remaining brother had started planning Alfred's resurrection themselves, after which, they planned to live in his brother's house on Church Road. They had just wanted a 'happily ever after' together, but that had been taken away from them when his brother had been killed in the church graveyard in January. Now Alfred was a homeless orphan once again with no living relatives at all.

"The baker's daughter is going to pay." Alfred said loudly and cursed the name of Jane Rose. Then the remnants of the child left within him checked that no one had overheard. His body was thirteen-years-old, but his mind was one-hundred-and-thirteen-years-old and tortured by the one-hundred-years that he had been trapped. He blamed Jane, the baker's daughter, for the death of his brother. It was Jane that had ruined his plan. She freed the other girl, Ginny, and then Jack's father had killed Alfred's

29

brother. Jack and Ginny were going to pay as well. They were all going to pay.

Alfred seethed inside as he remembered how the town had mocked him after his death—called him the shame of Middle Gratestone—while not showing shame at all. Instead they had lavished luxuries on the living, including those that were descended from his killers, rewarding them for the terrible deeds carried out by their ancestors.

"I'm not the shame of Middle Gratestone anymore," he said out loud. "I'm not anyone's shame. I'm Alfred. Alfred the destroyer of Middle Gratestone... no. Alfred the slayer of Middle Gratestone... no. Alfred the revenger of Middle Gratestone. No! Hmm, Alfred... the destructor, the—" he stopped and thought. Who was he? What was he? Was he actually alive? Really alive, like everyone else? But how could that be when he had been dead for so long. Maybe he was still dead? Maybe he was a ghost, a living ghost perhaps? The ghost of Middle Gratestone? Maybe that's what he was. Death hadn't exactly resurrected him but had instead somehow created a living ghost. Yes, that was it, that's what he was, a ghost with a living body. The ghost of Middle Gratestone. And he would have his revenge!

"They're going to suffer like I have suffered." Alfred smiled. Planning revenge always lifted his mood. He had planned revenge for the century that he had festered in the statue while time poisoned his soul. And now, with the warm weather and vengeance on his mind, Alfred felt happier than he had in a long while. First though, before he did anything else, he had to get off this farm. That meant he had to deal with Fat Joe. He continued walking away from the barn in a straight line, kicking the heads off dandelions as he went.

He headed towards an isolated copse of trees, perched on a knoll that rose from the fields like a hair-tufted wart. He was excited to see the spiders that gathered in the old, dried out water-well that was hidden in the copse. They waited there, catching the insects that buzzed through, safe in the shade of the trees and the deep of the well.

Alfred arrived and acknowledged the crows roosting silently in the trees with a nod then peered down, over the stone wall, into blackness. The spiders rustled in welcome. Warm, sickly air wafted out while the blackness inside moved in ripples around the walls.

Alfred felt the power that their numbers gave them. There were hundreds of them in there, maybe even thousands. They gathered in the well out of sight and waited in the darkness. Each bore a grey skull pattern on their black backs—a death mask that they carried with them and displayed in warning. Their legs and bodies were black and hairless, and their legs sleek and pointed with a hint of red underneath. They looked fast, agile and strong. They looked dangerous.

They were here because Alfred had called out to them. They heard him, and they came from miles around and gathered here in the well. They came to the boy that had died and they were ready to do whatever he needed them to do... but not yet.

Alfred opened his mind and felt them with his thoughts. He tried to connect with them and bid them to move, but they just gathered and waited. Something more was needed from him for them to submit fully to his will, but Alfred didn't know what that something was. He could sense them, but he couldn't command them. Not like before when he was dead. Something was missing. Something that he needed to bend them to his will. Alfred pondered, about what it could be that they needed from him? What was he missing?

While he was thinking, he reached out to them. He teased them with visions of what they could do together and showed them glimpses of his strength of mind. They submitted to him. They bound themselves to him, and he sensed they would do whatever he asked them to do. Even if it meant their own death. Even if it caused death. They would do anything for him, but not yet. For now, they resisted his will and they waited.

Chapter 7

Ginny walked up Church Road. She had planned on turning right at the end to go home, but she had a strange feeling of being followed, so instead, she walked slowly past her house, turned right at the school and continued to the parade of shops. No one was in at home but here there were people, so Ginny felt safer. She bought a lemonade and settled on a metal bench that circled a birch tree overlooking the shops.

Faceless people walked by as Ginny sipped her lemonade and stared straight ahead. Cars passed, but Ginny had no recollection of their colour the moment they were gone. She looked down and studied the minutia of the world at her feet. Cobblestones ringed the tree and bench, on which she sat, rising from concrete filled valleys that fixed them in concentric circles. A column of ants marched along the valleys and congregated around a pool of crushed, part-melted sweet. The ants took a small sticky piece each and trooped back, against the oncoming ants, along the same valley on which they had arrived.

Some ants were stuck to the sweet because they had got too close and were now trapped in the sticky mess. They were left there to die by their colleagues and no attempt at all was made to free them. Life in the colony was all about what was best for the many and not for the few.

"So, who should I leave behind?" Ginny asked the ants that were safely trooping back to their nest. "Who is our weakest member? Dave thinks he's strong, but he's scared. Jack normally knows what to do, but he seems lost. Jane keeps the peace but who needs peace? We need action."

Ginny looked at the trapped ants and tried to decide who she should leave behind to die. "Death wants one of us to die, that's clear from the dreams... but who? And what if nobody dies? What happens then?" she sighed then blew at the ants, but her breath dissipated before reaching them.

"You guys are not very helpful," she added, looking up and wondering if anyone had seen her talking to herself. A lady carrying flowerpots balanced in each hand walked hurriedly by on the other side of the road without looking around. She was reflected in the black windows of the Chinese takeaway for a moment as she passed. Ginny's eyes followed her then froze on the windows as the lady, struggling with the weight of the pots, moved on. Reflected in the windows, Ginny could see the road, the tree she was under and herself sat on the bench, but behind the tree everything was black.

She puzzled over it for a moment, thinking of the black mist that had chased her down in her dreams. Then she felt a cold dampness on her neck.

No! This can't be real, she thought, and looked down.

"I'm awake," she reassured herself turning her hands over and studying them, then checking herself all over. Her legs were there, her body was all complete, she wasn't in pain, and she wasn't in the throes of death. She noticed in front of her that the column of ants had melted away into

34

nothing, only those trapped in the sticky sweet remained. Ginny continued to look down, perhaps if she didn't acknowledge the dark mass behind her then it wouldn't be there.

But then she felt her aggression rise. This wasn't fair! Death was only meant to come in her dreams. Daytime was hers and she wasn't going to let Death have it.

"No!" she screamed and jumped to her feet, turning aggressively to fight the mist lurking in the bushes, if that was even possible. If she could even hope to do anything to something that had no substance.

Birds in the tree above her called out in alarm at the sudden commotion and the trees and bushes rustled as small animals took cover, but there was no mist.

"Are you alright dear?" an old lady asked. She looked like she needed help herself. She was ash-white and practically dead on her feet. Her cheekbones were pointed under her dried-out skin and her cheeks hollow, but she freely offered her assistance to Ginny anyway. Ginny recovered her control sufficiently to reply.

"No thank you, just a bee or a fly or something—it scared me."

"Okay then," the old lady smiled, a knowing smile, and continued slowly on. "You're a little young to be seeing him... watch out dear," she threw over her shoulder.

"Wait. What?" Ginny replied to the old lady's hunched, bent-over back. But she knew who the lady was talking about and the old lady knew that she knew, so continued walking without turning. She had other things to do with the little time that she had left.

Ginny stared at the old lady for a moment then looked around nervously. There was tension in the air. She wasn't sure if it meant a storm was coming or something deadlier, but the bench she had sat at didn't look welcoming at all now. She turned around two or three times on the spot looking for somewhere to go that was not exposed to danger, but there was nowhere so she started walking back in the direction from which she had come.

A group of crows hung around on an old stone wall next to the path. They eyed her, turning their heads one-by-one, to keep her in sight as she passed. Ginny knew a group of crows was called a 'murder' of crows. She shuddered then stepped away from them towards the road, then stepped into the road. She just caught the sound of a car coming as she did and threw herself back onto the path. The car beeped its horn and the crows mockingly cawed in laughter as they took flight.

Ginny leant on the wall to catch her breath and dislodged a small piece of the cement-pointing that held the stone wall together. She was suddenly wary it could collapse and stepped away to the centre of the path to be equally distant from the wall and road. The street corner by the school was just up ahead so she hurried forwards. As she reached it she heard footsteps running at full pelt, heavy footsteps, approaching from around the corner, so she stepped out of the way just as Dave rounded the corner at full speed.

"Death's coming!" he shouted as he saw her but didn't stop. "He can haunt us when we're awake," he continued. "Run!"

Ginny watched Dave pound away on the path along which she had just walked, until he disappeared around the next corner. But she didn't run. She didn't see the point. If Death was haunting them in the daytime now, then Death could find them anywhere.

I'm not going to run, she decided. I'm not going to hide... not ever! In that moment Ginny determined that she was not going to be cowed by Death. Whatever was thrown at her, whatever Death did to her... she would not be intimidated. She wouldn't run, and she wouldn't hide. She was Ginny Petherbridge and she would face Death down. It was time to take back control. So, for the second time that day she headed for the graveyard; after all there was no better place to confront Death than surrounded by dead people.

Perfect, she thought, and carried on towards the church with the confident stride of someone who had made up their mind.

Chapter 8

Jack and Jane walked around the church to the front path and stopped where they thought Alfred had died one-hundred-years ago. Jack cast his eyes around but there was no obvious sign of exactly where Alfred had fallen; no small plaque or tended flowers to mark the spot where he had drawn his last breath.

Jack looked at Jane. "Why do you think Alfred blames us for his death? It's not like we'd even been born when he died."

Jane shrugged nonchalantly, but then noted Jack's serious tone and tried to put her mind to answering his question. "My dad has some sort of family secret about it, as if he knows more than he's saying. But other than telling me our family has a debt to pay—he's told me nothing. I tried to worm it out of him once because he is always so secretive about it—but he wouldn't tell me."

"Yeah, me too, I sometimes think we're the only ones that don't know the whole story."

"Yes, you're right. I think that as well. I suppose I get that Alfred wanted to exchange one of our lives for his. He was just a kid when he died, and we're the kids around here so he wanted to take his revenge on us, that sort of makes sense. I kind of get the numbers thing as well. After all the dying and the coming back to life that happened that night. For Ginny to be brought back to life someone had to die— that was the old Alfred, Alfred Thatcher... he died so that's balanced. But then for Alfred, the shame, to be brought back to life someone else had to die as well, but nobody did. So, it's not balanced that's why Death is chasing us now. I get it. But it still sucks."

"You're not wrong there," Jack agreed.

"And what if we just get on and live our lives and die later of old age? What's the problem with that? Why does Death want to rebalance things so urgently?"

"Maybe we'll never know that Jane. I think the real question though is can we live like this? Can we accept being killed every night in our dreams? Because I don't think that I can. I stay awake longer and longer at night to avoid dreaming. But living without sleep is not living at all. It's too hard. I'm exhausted Jane and I don't know how much longer I can go on like this."

"Jack, you can tell me about your dream if you want to. I won't judge you or think bad of you. They're dreams created by Death not by you." Jane said gently, not looking at Jack until she finished. Then she half looked him in the eye and looked away quickly after, so as not to spook him.

"Thanks," Jack replied, knowing that he would never tell Jane about his dream. "Maybe I will one day."

Jane saw from the hardness in Jack's face that it would be a long time before he changed his mind and told her about his dream. "Do you think Dave would actually try to kill Ginny?" Jane changed the subject.

"I don't trust him," Jack replied instantly. "We already know he's willing to sacrifice me and Ginny. It's not such a big step from that to actually trying to kill one of us."

"Yeah of all of us he's probably the one most likely to try."

"Unless Ginny thinks the same and tries to kill him first... get him before he gets her, sort of thing."

"Yeah, all the drama is going to involve those two... we're okay though aren't we Jack?"

"Yes, we are." Jack forced a smile to hide what he thought. "Do you fancy a posh coffee?" he asked, thinking it was his turn to change the subject.

"Oh yeah—let's do the Café Shack. I need cake and caffeine." Jane hoisted her bag and tucked her arm into Jack's. They walked towards town along the same route Ginny had walked earlier but turned left at the school and ducked into the Café Shack—their usual weekend treat place.

The shack was about half full. It smelt gloriously of roast coffee beans and sounded of low happy conversation and chinking cups and mugs. They ordered drinks and cakes then Jack sat down while Jane went to the ladies' room tucked away at the back of the café.

"Back in a sec," she told him.

Jack sat facing towards the long window that looked out onto the street, so he could keep an eye on who came and went. He rested his forearms on the polished dark wood table, leaving a gap between his arms large enough to receive coffee and cake. Nameless jazz music, playing just under the sound of voices, filled the café with a constant hubbub but he didn't listen.

Jack worried, as he always did these days. He tried to think the problem through. He liked to apply a bit of logic to all problems, but this one was proving to be particularly difficult to solve. Jane killed him every night in his dreams, but that was Death's direction of his dream not Jane's. So, what did Death mean by it? Did he mean that Jane should kill Jack, or that she would kill Jack? Or the opposite... did he mean Jack should kill Jane? Perhaps it was a warning to Jack that if he didn't kill Jane then she would kill him?

The only thing clear was Death's message at the end of the dream—delivered in Jack's inner voice—that the balance was wrong and one of them should die. But why was Jack's dream different to everyone else's? Why was everyone else killed by Death and not killed by Jane? That part did not make sense yet, unless Jack had some pivotal role in Death's plan. Still at least it was only a dream...

Jack slowly became aware of Jane stood to his right, so he looked up inquisitively—normally she would sit right away. She was stood side-on looking down at him, her face devoid of expression. Jack looked deep into her eyes. They were glassy and dead looking.

Dead looking!

Jack flinched but otherwise stayed in place. Horror and shock froze his limbs, as he desperately looked deep into

41

Jane's dead eyes. Is she dead? Jack thought. But she's standing up!

Jane sidestepped to her right to gain a little space between them, then hoisted and swung the huge bone-handled scythe that she had been shielding from Jack's view. It cleaved the coffee table in two pieces that wobbled then separated. The half on which Jack's forearms rested remained vertical; the half with his hands fell forward, taking his hands with it. Jack screamed! The sound cut through the hubbub in the café. Somewhere a cup fell and smashed.

"Oh my!" a lady gasped and raised a hand to her mouth. Everybody in the café turned to look at Jack in shock while Jane yanked on the scythe to pull the point out of the floorboards in which it was embedded, but it wouldn't come, so she started working it back and forwards.

Jack looked at the stumps where his hands had been. They were neatly cut through and blood came from both in synchronised spurts. He jumped up and ran before Jane could free the scythe. He reached the door in a few strides but was held up as he struggled to work the door handle with his elbows. Blood spurting from his stumps coated the door handle making it slippery and he started to panic. A bemused looking elderly gentleman reached across and opened it for him.

Why is everyone looking at me? Jack thought as he rushed outside. Why aren't they looking at the crazy girl with the scythe? Then he realised... they couldn't see her! She wasn't there!

Jack looked down at his stumps and saw his hands back in place. Then he looked up and saw Jane was gone and the table was in one piece exactly where it was before. The realisation that Death was now haunting Jack in the daytime slowly dawned on him.

"Sorry," he blurted out to the customers then turned and ran.

Chapter 9

The noise of the hand dryer, blasting the water off Jane's hands, drowned out Jack's scream. Jane finished off drying her hands on her denim jeans then checked herself in the mirror, oblivious to his torment.

"Still ugly," she told herself, mourning the loss of her long hair then with a sigh she produced a brush from her bag and ran it through what was left. Not to style it, but because it paid to check her hair for bugs after being outside.

While she brushed, Jane saw the bruised and battered young girl looking out at her again, so she turned away to avoid the accusing stare. 'Look at what you've done to me,' the eyes reflected in the mirror said to her. 'I used to be beautiful but your neurotic obsession with bugs has made me ugly. Look at me now. Look at my hair—what's left of it. How could you cut it all off? I hate you.'

She rummaged through her bag to distract from the harsh judgement and found an aerosol can.

"Eau de fly spray?" she offered herself.

"Oh yes please... perfect," she answered sarcastically for her mirror image, delivering a squirt to each side of her neck and each wrist.

"I hope it doesn't repel Jack." That was one thing she and her mirror image agreed upon. Jane looked at herself one last time, shrugged in disappointment, then turned and left. With a bit of luck, she wouldn't have to look at herself again until tomorrow morning.

The scene in the café surprised her when she returned. Firstly, everyone in the café stopped talking and stared at her; secondly, Jack was not at the table on which their coffees idly steamed. Jane unconsciously brushed at her hair with a hand then ran her hands down her front, expecting something was wrong with her appearance, but found nothing amiss. She pulled out her chair and sat down, facing towards the back of the café, away from all the staring eyes, annoyed at herself for the instant red flush that appeared around her neck and gave away her discomfort.

Just behind her, a chair squealed backwards on the floor then a woman appeared at Jane's side. "I don't think he's coming back love," she said as kindly as she could.

Jane nodded. "I'll wait," she half smiled, and half looked at the woman. Cheap perfume filled her nostrils, so she tried to keep her mouth shut to stop herself from tasting it as well—although her eau de fly spray probably smelt worse. "Thank you," Jane added to encourage the woman to leave but she didn't seem ready to go.

"He let out an almighty scream then ran out—he looked terrified—like he'd seen a ghost... probably on drugs... you're not on drugs are you dear?" she fussed.

"No, of course not," Jane replied, but didn't look up. She really didn't want to hear whatever the woman seemed determined to tell her about Jack.

"Alright my love," the woman took the hint and moved off leaving Jane alone in her disquiet.

Jane waited for the chair behind her to slide back into place and the woman and her companion to revive their conversation, then she looked around using mirrors and as much of her side vision as she could. People gradually stopped staring and quietly returned to their drinks and conversations and slowly the sound level returned to normal.

Jane picked at her apple pie—it wasn't as good as Jack's Grandmother's apple pie—but it was apple pie nonetheless. The coffee was hot and rich, so she sipped at it while deciding what to do. On the other side of the table Jack's coffee mug loomed over her like a stone memorial. She tried to avoid looking at it, so she wouldn't have to face the truth it represented. But there was no getting away from it— Jack had left and all she could do was mourn his departure.

I'll give him five minutes, she thought, then I'm going home.

Chapter 10

Jack slowed to a jog then broke into a walk and looked around warily as he headed towards his house. He glanced down Church Road as he passed but it was quiet. He felt a bit silly now and wondered what Jane would think of him for running out? And what the people in the café had thought? He stopped at a tree and leant on the wall behind it to gather his thoughts.

It was quiet in the street, so Jack let his breathing slow down and thought about Jane.

I left her, he worried. She's alone in the café wondering what happened to me.

But in his heart Jack knew that it was better that he was apart from Jane. It was bad enough being killed by Jane in his sleep but now to be killed by Jane when he was awake— that was too much to take. He looked at his wrists where Jane had severed them and shuddered. It had seemed so real. He had seen Jane cut his hands off at the wrist. He had felt the blade cut through and the warm blood splash over him. The searing pain as his flesh was exposed to the air— the shock—the agony. How could it have felt so real and yet be an illusion?

Jack clasped his hands to his forehead trying to squeeze out the horror. What if he started to become scared of Jane? What if he couldn't tell the real Jane apart from the Jane of Death?

Pounding feet interrupted his thoughts so he peered out from his hiding place and saw Dave running away from him towards the school. Nervously, Jack pulled back away from the road again and sunk against the wall behind the tree. Only one thing could have scared Dave into running like that, he thought, and that was Death.

Dave must have had a Death experience as well, surmised Jack. So that's what Death is doing to us now. That's the answer to whether things can get worse. Yes, they can because now Death is haunting us while we're awake as well as when we're asleep.

"Jack?" Jane called softly from the other side of the tree. Jane's voice startled him and he pulled forward to see her. She was ready for him and immediately swung the scythe in an arc at waist height. It cut straight through him and sunk deep into the tree. Jack grabbed at the tree and held onto a branch as his balance deserted him then his legs stepped sideways and toppled over leaving his torso hanging from the tree.

He couldn't scream, the searing pain across his middle took his breath away, he gasped and choked but couldn't get air into his lungs. He looked around in panic as Jane ripped the scythe out of the tree and swung it again cutting through Jack's right arm at the shoulder, his head just above the jaw and his left arm. Half his head separated from his torso and both dropped to the ground leaving his arms hanging from the tree.

Jack opened his eyes and sucked in the air, his face was in the thick green grass that lined the path. He pushed himself to his knees and gorged on the rich air. Energy and life flooded through him in a euphoric rush of realisation.

"I'm alive!" he cried out as he checked his arms and legs, by patting himself down. He looked around for Jane and just caught sight of her behind him as she swung the scythe. It took the top of his head off like a split coconut and the top piece span in the air and landed in front of him. He fell forward onto it and heard his own inner voice in his head. It spoke to him, but they were Death's words—not Jack's.

"Two living and one dead. The balance is wrong. It must be restored."

Once again, Jack came-to with his face in the grass. He froze for a second as he collected his thoughts but then the truth overwhelmed him. Jane had killed him! Although the agony of the attack had passed, the emotional pain lingered like a blistered burn. Why was Death torturing him disguised as Jane? It was unbearable, it was too much to take and he had to stop it somehow. Then, before Jane could attack again, he thrusted himself forward like a sprinter bursting from the blocks and ran for his life.

Chapter 11

Alfred only stayed at the well for ten minutes then hurried back to the barn so as not to give Fat Joe any reason to come looking for him. He tutted as he walked past the plough that he had cleaned yesterday. He had spent all day brushing off the mud, hosing it clean and applying oil to joints so that it could be put away.

All Fat Joe had to do was hitch the plough to his tractor and move it into the barn, but he hadn't even been bothered to do that. Alfred stared at the plough. It made him angry that it was still there because it should be inside now, shiny and clean, not outside waiting to rust. The months that he had spent working on the farm had built his confidence and strength. He had thrown himself into the endless tasks that Fat Joe had given him and now he believed that he could run the farm better than Fat Joe.

Maybe when he looked older, people would take him seriously; it wasn't easy being one-hundred-and-thirteen-years-old in a thirteen-year-old body. Perhaps, after he had revenged his family, he could come back here and takeover the farm. Alfred liked that idea—all he needed was a plan. He carried on walking past the barn.

At the rough centre of the farm, a cobblestone courtyard separated the farmhouse from the stables and outbuildings. The stables held the tractor, some old rusted cars and various junk items like fridges and washing machines that should have been thrown out but had been left to rust instead. Doors to the stable hung loose from their hinges and planks that had loosened clung onto sidewalls held in place by the scarce few nails that were left.

Across the courtyard, the dirty farmhouse was in even worse condition than the stables. Peeling scabs of plaster-rending hung from its walls ready to slough onto the floor, tiles were missing from the roof like gapped teeth and weeds hung down from the rotten window sills and crooked guttering. It looked sick, blighted by age and neglect. If it were a family pet, kindness would have euthanised it long ago rather than allowing its suffering to continue.

Alfred crossed the courtyard, looking down at his feet while pondering his future. There must be a way to get everything he wanted, he thought, as he picked his way through rubbish on the garden path that led to the farmhouse door.

A piece of paper hung on the door from a nail half-banged into the wood. Fat Joe stuck a job list on the nail every evening so that it would be there for Alfred when he got up in the morning. Alfred looked at it:

'*Fix the fence. Nails and hammer in the tool shed.*'

Alfred hadn't been allowed in the tool shed before. Fat Joe is getting careless, he thought. Maybe there's something in there that I can use to help me escape from here.

On the farmhouse doorstep was a glass of water. Two flies bobbed around in it; one dead and one panicking, franticly kicking around in circles. Next to the glass, a curled sandwich sat on a white china plate. Alfred scooped out the flies from the glass and flicked his hand, so they sailed off into the long grass that lined the path, then he drank the water in quick thirsty gulps. He set the glass down carefully on the step then picked up the sandwich and tucked it in his pocket; there were nicer places on the farm to eat than here.

After a quick furtive look around, he decided he was not being watched so he ambled around the side of the farmhouse, stepping over upturned buckets and skirting several piles of rotting unidentifiable matter. He could see the shed alongside the house. Weeds and dirt grew up the sides of the shed as if the ground was attempting to swallow it whole. The padlock was hanging loose from the hasp on the door. Alfred unhooked it and creaked the door open. He took the padlock in with him so that no one could lock him inside and placed it on the shelf nearest the door.

Every wall inside the shed was tiered with shelves, on which were stacked rusted tools, old paint tins and an array of junk that would befit an antique shop. With a gasp of pleasant surprise, Alfred recognised them. He was more familiar with the contents of this shed than the TV's, computers and phones that littered Fat Joe's farmhouse. He was after all one-hundred-and-thirteen-years-old. He recognised the tools as like those that his father had owned. There were old chisels, wooden-handled planes, hammers, handsaws and a complete range of old worn files.

For a moment, Alfred felt at home, as if he had just walked into his father's workshop. He remembered the smell of fresh cut oak and recalled the rasping of his father's handsaw. He saw him laughing and joking with his other son, Alfred's older brother, and for the first time in a long time, Alfred smiled a genuine happy smile that lifted his soul out from the abyss in which it perpetually wallowed.

He took a brass hand-drill from a shelf and turned the handle. It was stiff but then it loosened and squeaked into life. The squeak reminded him of his dad carefully drilling, with his tongue poking out in concentration, as the drill cut into the wood.

'Measure twice, cut once,' his dad had advised him.

Alfred's smile fell away, and he cried. Tears rolled down his cheeks as he stood in the middle of the shed turning the handle of the hand-drill and remembering his family that had been torn from him. His family that had been killed by the murderers that lived in Middle Gratestone. His family that he so wanted back but couldn't. His hand started to slow and the time between the squeaks got longer and longer until they finally stopped. Alfred placed the drill gently on the shelf exactly where it had been before and wiped the wet from his cheeks. He wouldn't let Fat Joe have the satisfaction of seeing his tears.

The nails and hammer were next to each other on a shelf near the door. Alfred gathered them up and put them in a tool bag. Then he collected his thoughts and left the tool shed.

The orchard was the other side of the farmhouse. Alfred entered over a broken-down wall and scrunched himself up in the shade of an old apple tree. It was probably beautiful in here once but now it was overgrown with weeds within the crumbling walls. Nature had started to reclaim this part of the farm but it suited Alfred just fine.

The sandwich in his pocket needed a little brushing off before he could eat it, but between the slices of bread was a thick slice of smoked ham that smelled delicious. Alfred ate slowly and savoured the taste as he thought about why he could still feel and communicate with the spiders but couldn't control them anymore.

He thought back to when he had been trapped in the statue, unable to leave, unable to live his life, just trapped there as the world moved on. He had watched children walk happily by, on the path next to the graveyard while he was trapped. He had watched the children grow up over the years and become adults that then had children of their own. All the while he was jealous of the life that they were living, and he was not.

The cycle had continued for one-hundred-years while Alfred raged in frustration—neither living nor dead—trapped in the statue that was sculpted in his own likeness. As years passed and his rage grew Alfred started to sense the wildlife around him. He knew they were there before he saw them, and he became adept at identifying them by how they felt in his mind. Slowly, the connection he had with the small creatures that scurried around the graveyard became stronger until he could influence what they did and to the point when he could bend them to his will and command them to do what he wanted.

Then finally the last piece of the puzzle had fallen into place and Alfred had learnt how to poison the creatures and use them to bite people and infect them so that they then changed into monstrous creatures themselves that he could use to take his revenge. His giant spiders had brought Jack to the graveyard and lured Jane and Ginny so that Alfred could kill one of them and take their place amongst the living. But it hadn't gone to plan and instead of one of the stupid kids ending up dead, Alfred's brother had died, and Alfred took his brother's place amongst the living.

Ever since then though, Alfred had lost his ability to control spiders, rats, bats, foxes and all the other creatures of the night. He couldn't even influence them anymore, he could only feel their presence. They continued to help him though, like the spider that had tapped out the warning of Fat Joe's arrival in the barn earlier. That gave Alfred hope that maybe the connection would strengthen again, like before when he was trapped in the statue. Maybe it would strengthen, and he could command an army of creatures that would descend on Middle Gratestone and wipe out the town that had destroyed his life. Yes, maybe....

Alfred stopped his musing, stood up, grabbed the tool bag and headed out to the farm perimeter to start fixing the fence. It was a good job to do, he thought. The fence was the furthest part of the farm away from the farmhouse and from Fat Joe. That meant that he could relax and work in peace.

The ground was flat in the valley and the grass had been kept short by the cows that meandered around in a tight herd. He stretched his legs and walked quickly while he did some maths in his head. The farm was about one square mile, so each side was one mile long, so that's four miles, he calculated. Plus, the fences that sectioned up the inside into separate enclosures; that made maybe eight miles of fence in total. This job was going to take a while he thought, but that was good—he'd be away from Fat Joe for days.

It took ten minutes for Alfred to reach the outer fence and another ten to find a corner to start from. Once there, Alfred walked slowly away from the corner and strolled alongside the fence, kicking and pushing at it every now and then to check for any loose planks. He spotted one that had dropped at one end, so he lifted it back into place and braced it with his hip then positioned a nail and banged it in—two soft strikes and two hard—just as his dad had taught him. Alfred inspected the nail head that was now flush with the wood and moved on, satisfied with his work.

Three fenceposts down he found another loose plank, so he banged the existing nail home and then added one of his own for good measure. The work became regular, monotonous even. Walk a bit, bang a nail in, walk a bit, bang a nail in. A light sheen of sweat developed on his brow as he worked steadily, and his mind drifted to more important matters.

Why couldn't he control the spiders? What if he could never control the spiders again? What was missing? He looked at his hands. He was flesh and blood now—not a ghost trapped in a statue anymore. Maybe he could only control the spiders when he was dead? But it didn't feel like that. It felt like the spiders were waiting and if they were waiting then there must be a way to get his power back.

He sensed one up ahead. He could feel it like a presence in his own mind. A growing awareness of the spider as he closed the distance to where it hung in its web. As he got closer he sensed what the spider could see. What it could feel. There was no danger here, the spider knew that. It waited patiently for prey to drift in on the wind; it waited and watched. Alfred stopped walking when he reached the web. It was large and thick, spanning two slats and was nestled in the lee of a fencepost for protection. Alfred knew the spider was not hungry and he knew it was female and that new life was growing inside her. She sensed Alfred and reared up on her back legs in welcome.

"Hello beautiful," Alfred said. He crouched down and took in the detail of her brown plump abdomen and long slender legs. He flicked his eyes from the spider to the outer edge of the web, willing the spider to move to where his eyes pointed.

Move, he commanded with a thought. He felt resistance. The spider wouldn't do it.

Move, he commanded again. Nothing.

Alfred stared. He could crush the spider, but that was not his way.

"Go in peace friend," he said and moved on. Two posts further down a plank hung loose. Alfred readied a nail.

Chapter 12

The top hinge of the church gate had been broken for a long time, causing the gate to droop and scrape on the path, creating a deep semi-circular score in the tarmac. The gate's bottom corner was now jammed at the end of the score. Ginny stepped into the semicircle and took a moment to survey the church and graveyard; not to find beauty in it as Jane had tried earlier by the stream, but to find danger. There could be lots of creatures here that would do her harm: Death, giant spiders, Dave? Experience told her this is where they gathered. She tugged at the gate to make sure it was securely jammed and wouldn't get in the way if she had to leave in a hurry later, then stepped into the graveyard.

Her heartbeat was raised. Not through fear, but through nervous excitement—Ginny felt good to be doing something—it was doing nothing that scared her. She looked hard into the shaded areas of the graveyard: under trees, behind gravestones, and in the wet, mildewed corners of the church walls that the sun had not touched for centuries—anywhere that provided a source for the dark mist that was Ginny's version of Death. She thought through what she knew about Death as she walked—to see if she could find something that she could use to her advantage, or perhaps even solve the mystery of why she and the others were being haunted.

Death could be seen, Death could speak in her head, Death could appear in her dreams and Death could kill her in her dreams. But after she had been killed she woke up and nothing was wrong—there was no lasting effect. So, logically then, maybe in daylight it was all just an illusion. Maybe Death couldn't do any of them any actual harm.

Ginny had an idea that she thought might help to find out. She pottered about, walking around gravestones, careful to avoid the raised mounds of earth that stretched out from the foot of the stones. Some mounds were earthy, some grassed over, and some sunken with age and woven with weeds. Ginny respectfully skirted them all as she scouted out the dark spots of the graveyard and peered into shadows.

She circled the church, once round in a rough circle, then turned and retraced her steps to the back of the church and headed for the oldest part of the graveyard down by the stream. There were more statues here, where the graveyard slunk under the weeping willows that hid the stream from view. The statues were spread out, facing in odd directions unlike any crowd of real people ever would, and the large weeping willows guarded the graveyard perimeter keeping the statues hemmed in.

Ginny approached the willow furthest to the left and eyed it warily. The heavily leafed branches hung down to knee height and formed a thick curtain around the tree, shielding the interior from view. Without hesitation, she put her right arm through the curtain. It was cold inside. It felt like she was shaking hands with a dead person. The grip though, was limp and it clung to her like a web floating in the breeze, lank and uncertain as it wafted around her outstretched arm.

Ginny held her hand in place and gritted her teeth, waiting for something to yank her in. It felt like a rite of passage, like something that she had to do to gain entry. A test to be passed before the tree would reveal its secrets. Ginny held firm—seconds passed, and nothing happened, so she pulled the curtain aside and peered through. The dark shade inside was hued green from the sun that filtered through the leaves. Ginny stepped in and released the curtain. It swung back in place, allowing the shade to fill the dome under the tree.

As her eyes adjusted to the dim, she could see the trunk that supported the grand old willow and behind the trunk the stream that gurgled past. The branches on the far side of the willow dipped into the river, completing the dome, and collecting twigs that floated within reach. Ginny circled the trunk carefully, holding onto it for support on the streamside, so she didn't slip into the water because although the stream was shallow her white tennis shoes were new.

She started to relax. There was nothing here and now her eyes were adjusted she appreciated how beautiful and refreshing it was in the cool shade. She began to feel secure inside the trees comforting embrace, so she sat down and stretched her legs out in front of her. To complete the calming effect, she produced some chewing gum from a pocket and popped it into her mouth.

So, two living and one dead, the balance must be restored. Ginny mused over Death's words. Alfred had come back, I came back, old Alfred died. So... the result is two resurrections and one death. That's why we need another death, Ginny thought, then puffed out her cheeks and let out a sigh, reminded by her thoughts of the moment when she had given her life in the graveyard to save Jane.

"I've made my sacrifice already," she said out loud in the secrecy of the dome. "It's someone else's turn."

It was brave dying once for your friends, she considered, but dying twice for them was stupid. If someone must die to make Death leave them alone, then it wasn't going to be her. Not this time—not again.

Ginny recalled what it had been like dying in the snowy graveyard back in January. She had been alive then everything had just stopped. Later she had been brought back, but when she looked back on it and tried to recall what it felt like, the most unsettling thing was that she had been aware of the part when everything was stopped. Time hadn't just skipped from when she died to when she was alive again; she had been aware of the passing of time while she was dead. It was all she had been aware of. It had gone on and on forever, totally out of step with time passing in the world of the living.

Tick, tick, tick... time kept going and going and going. How could she possibly bear that forever? Was that death?

Nothing but time passing for all eternity? Her whole existence stopped forever while the world moved on. No sight, no sound, no thoughts? Ginny shivered, then shivered again from the cold that crept up her back.

Dark tendrils of black fog started to swim around her like ink spreading out in water. It froze her skin where it touched her and killed the sparse grass under the weeping willow in an instant. Ginny pushed away from the trunk and leapt to her feet. She backed up against the curtain of leaves but didn't push through. Instead she pulled out her phone and started filming the black mist as it flowed up the bank towards her.

She glanced between the screen and the blackness in front of her. It was there, both in the clearing and on the screen. Ginny looked at the screen again and saw a figure come out of the mist. It floated just off the ground, gliding up the bank with the mist, on legs that didn't move. Ginny looked up from her phone straight into the figure's black, dead eyes—Jane's black, dead eyes.

"Jane," she stammered, completely aghast, then Jane reached her and put her outstretched hands around Ginny's neck and squeezed hard. The front of Ginny's throat collapsed under the pressure of Jane's tight grip and shut off her airway. The tendrils of mist poured into her eyes and her mouth, filling her with cold darkness.

It overwhelmed her. It buried her under muddy earth in an unmarked grave. It dragged her under the ocean down into the deep where light never reached and held her there under the crushing weight of the water above. It put out the light of her life and cast it into the black abyss where it could never be found.

Blood stopped flowing to Ginny's brain and she lapsed into unconsciousness just before her neck cracked loudly as it snapped.

Ginny opened her eyes, but the sun burnt into them. She looked away and sat up quickly while sucking in air with a gasp and blinking away the image of the sun. She was half-in half-out of the willow tree. "Jane," she coughed and felt her neck. It was sore but not crushed as she remembered it had been just before she had lost consciousness. She rolled onto her knees, still feeling the effects of her encounter then remembered her phone. It wasn't in her hand. She couldn't see it, so she crawled under the willow tree and found it lying on the ground. It was still recording.

After stopping the video, Ginny played it back and watched carefully, fascinated by what she had recorded. The video showed the tree trunk but no black mist and no floating Jane. She watched it through to the end, until she heard herself choking then falling through the curtain of willow branches. But there was still no mist and no Jane.

"Okay so it was all in my head." Ginny concluded. No matter how real it seemed at the time, it wasn't, it was an illusion and Death was never here. But Jane? Where did she come from? Was that a message? Was Jane going to kill her? Was Death warning her?

The questions buzzed around in her head as she left the interior of the weeping willow and headed back through the graveyard. She had a lot of thinking to do and the seed of a plan started to form in her mind.

Chapter 13

Jane spent a brutal twenty minutes in the Café Shack, during which she felt that the absent Jack and her, were discussed and judged by everyone in there. Quietly, the other customers passed harsh judgement on her, whispering at their tables just out of her earshot. She stayed there long enough for them to see that she wasn't afraid of them, that she wasn't rushing to leave and that she didn't care what their verdict might be. Then she calmly walked out, without giving any of them a second glance.

"Take care dear," said the woman that spoke to her earlier. It sounded like an order, not a pleasantry. Jane ignored her.

The café door closed on the jury's verdict and Jane breathed in the air outside. It was markedly fresher out here, so she took a couple of deep breaths to clear herself of the heavy café air then started to walk home. There was no sign of Jack, so she walked along trying to look like she wasn't looking for him as she looked for him.

She felt robbed. This should have been her opportunity to spend time with Jack. But instead of staring into his blue eyes, over coffee and cake, she had endured a trial and been found guilty by unanimous verdict of being an unwelcome patron of the Café Shack; a rough person, a druggie, an undesirable... one of the untrusted youth of today. She reeled off what the old people might call her:

hoodlum, ruffian, thug, lout. "Hah! Whatever." She said out loud.

Perhaps they would petition for her to be banned from the café in punishment, she thought.

She was also unsure as to whether she should be angry at Jack, or worried about him.

Worried, she decided. Angry would mean he had walked out on her for no reason—and that was not an acceptable possibility. Worried was better than angry even though it meant that something had happened to him.

But what? She wondered. She recalled the lady's words to her earlier.

'He looked like he had seen a ghost dear.'

Maybe it wasn't a ghost. Maybe it was Death that he had seen, Jane surmised.

She reached Church Road and looked for any sign of Jack, or anything else that might help her understand what was going on. Leafy trees lined either side, obscuring the church and many of the cottages, but allowing scattered glimpses through the branches of painted walls on one side and black weathered stone on the other. Jane took the path on the cottages side of the road, and strolled down—still not looking for Jack, anywhere that he might be.

Sunlight dappled the ground under the trees, writhing around as the gentle breeze swayed the branches above. Adjacent trees creaked against each other in the wind, as they slowly tried to raise their leafy branches above their neighbour and cover them in shade. Their fight was a long one, fought over years, and played out while people scurried about underneath, oblivious to the struggle for supremacy above.

Jane strolled on, thinking of her own struggle.

Is there a chance that Death would just leave if we do nothing? she wondered and glanced with the corner of her eye at a bench tucked back against the fence that lined the front gardens of the cottages. Nope, no Jack, she confirmed what she had expected, and walked on.

It was humid under the trees. Bees buzzed in the leafy canopy and charged the air with their wings, adding to the oppressive noise of the branches creaking and leaves rustling in the breeze. Jane felt uncomfortable and shrugged in her clothes trying to unstick them from her skin.

The sound of a stick tapping the fence posts crept into her consciousness. It was approaching from behind—maybe fifty-yards distant. It was rhythmic, tap-tap-tap...

Probably a child dragging a stick along the fence slats, she thought, while continuing to ponder about Death and surreptitiously checking behind trees for Jack.

The child was walking quicker than Jane so the gap started to close. Forty-yards, thirty-yards, twenty-yards... she looked back, but the tree trunks were in the way. Fifteen-yards, ten-yards... she looked back again, but still couldn't see anything, so she stepped towards the fence and looked back along the fence line. She saw that she had reached number seven Church Road, Alfred Thatcher's old cottage. The garden was overgrown around the 'For Sale' sign planted in the middle. But otherwise everything appeared normal.

The moment Jane had looked and saw that there was nobody there, the sound had stopped. Thinking that the child had stepped back onto the path, Jane also stepped back. Right in front of her, dappled in sunlight, stood her angel of death. Jane's breath caught in her throat and the blood drained from her face, causing her to look as white as the creature in front of her. The angel should only haunt her in her dreams!

The angel stood seven-feet-tall and looked down on Jane with eyes that were made of black mist swirling around inside her eye sockets. Her mouth was lipless, exposing teeth that were sharpened to points. Behind the teeth, the same black mist swirled as if she was filled with it. A battered breastplate covered her front, over which a great shawl was draped that floated around her. At her waist, an empty scabbard hung, and in her hand, was the sword that had been drawn from the scabbard.

The angel floated the last few feet towards Jane, dragging the sword along the fence slats as she came, tapping them out one-by-one, then stopped inches from Jane. They stood like that, frozen, facing each other. Jane decided she needed to fill the silence.

"What?" she asked then felt stupid. If she was going to talk to Death she might as well say something better than just 'what.'

"What do you want from me?" she elaborated. "Why can't you just leave me alone? What's so bad about there being no balance?" Jane looked in Death's eyes for an answer, but the mist that swirled there was deep, fathomless and cold.

And old! she thought. So old—like, the eyes had seen everything—everything that ever was and everything that had ever happened. Those eyes had been around since the beginning of the world, she saw. They had seen so much they had become ambivalent—uncaring. Life and death were now trifling matters of no importance after so much of them both had been endured again and again over millennia.

Death withdrew the sword from the fence and swapped it from her left hand to her right. The hands were shaped like talons, hooked and clawed, but they gripped just like human hands. The right talon held the sword on the blade, just below the hilt. Death stretched out an arm offering the sword, hilt first, to Jane.

"You want me to take it?" Jane asked and took a step back suspecting a trick, but the answer to her question was obvious. Death was handing the sword to her, just like her mother had passed her a bread baguette last night.

Jane looked at the sword held at arm's length, just in front of her. The hilt was bound in leather, held in place by shiny metal wire that twisted around the grip. On the end, was a pommel formed of black stone filled with shooting stars that zipped around inside. The guard, just above Death's talon, was formed of dull metal inlaid with runes that moved as Jane tried to focus on them. Under Death's talon, a black blade curved in a crescent that almost reached the floor. The blade looked sharp, dangerous and threatening.

Jane decided that it was better if she had the sword rather than leave it in Death's hands, so she reached out to take it.

"Not yet," Death said in Jane's voice inside her head. Jane flinched as Death invaded her mind and took over her inner voice. "Soon," the voice continued. Then the angel of death, swirled into a grey fog and dispersed. Jane's thoughts became her own once again, so she stepped back to avoid breathing in the fog, suddenly worried that it might poison her. The path and trees came back into view as the fog disappeared into nothing and within seconds there was no trace of Death. Jane was alone on the path, staring back up in the direction from which she had come.

"Jack!" she cried out, suddenly consumed by the need to find him. She marched back up the road to Jack's house where she hoped he might be, so that she could tell him what had just happened.

She walked quickly and looked around constantly, no longer worried about trying to look cool, or concealing her searching of the shadows on route. She had to find Jack and make sure he was okay, and she had to tell him about her encounter with Death.

At least I didn't get killed this time, she thought. But why would Death offer me her sword... and what did she mean by 'not yet?' There were just too many questions and not enough answers, she decided.

Jane turned into Jack's road and was relieved to see him sitting on the wall outside his house. It was a nice house, one of the early houses that formed the original village that had grown into the town of Middle Gratestone of today. The garden wall was old and made of huge chunks of stone cemented together. Jack often sat there; Jane remembered him sitting there with his dad, years ago when Jack was a young boy, and life had been simpler for them all.

Jane smiled at Jack from two-hundred-yards away, but he was looking down at his phone and wasn't aware of her yet. She checked around her, to make sure Death wasn't following and speeded up a little bit more. She was already breathing heavily from the brisk walk, but a little more speed would help her get the questions that were crashing against each other in her brain out into the open and answered, before she went mad from them.

"Jack!" she called as she closed on him.

Jack looked up, startled, almost falling off the wall. He caught his phone, which had shot up in the air, then he turned and jumped off the wall into his front garden, so that the wall was between him and Jane.

"Jack?" Jane called him again. Jack's head appeared over the wall as he looked at her warily. His eyes wide open, full of distrust and fear.

"Jack?" Jane repeated a third time.

"Jane?" Jack answered.

"Well this is a thrilling conversation!" Jane stopped ten-yards short of Jack. "What's wrong?" she asked. "Why did you leave the Café Shack? They said you screamed and ran out."

"Oh... sorry," Jack was still wary.

"Jack are you okay?" Jane walked slowly up to the wall, so that she didn't send him running.

"No," he blurted out. "No, I'm not okay. I got killed again... twice. I can't take this," his voice cracked. He rubbed at his face and peered through his fingers. When he lowered his hands, Jane could see they were shaking.

Jane stepped forward and took his hands in hers, holding them tight before he could object, or pull away. The wall between them felt like a mental barrier as well as a physical one. And it was growing. Jane sensed Jack slipping away from her, shutting down his emotions, building a wall between them as strong as the one they were straddling.

Jack sniffed, and his voice wavered. "What's happening Jane? Why are we being hunted down like this? Why do you—" Jack shook his head "—why does Death keep killing me?"

"I don't know Jack," Jane wanted to hold him, but the wall was in the way. She hadn't noticed Jack's near slip of the tongue, so she pressed on with her own story. "I've just seen Death as well, my angel of death. But she didn't kill me this time."

"What?" questioned Jack, in surprise.

"She held out her sword and offered it to me, but when I went to take it, she said 'not yet.' What do you think that means?"

"She offered you her sword?" Jack looked horrified. "Don't take it Jane. Whatever you do, don't take it."

"Why not? It's better for me to have it than her."

"Is it Jane? What will you do with it?"

"Well I don't know. I guess I thought it would stop her killing me... and maybe I could use it myself."

"What! Are you going to kill people with it?"

"No, of course not... maybe I'll use it on Death, that's all. Why are you being like this?" Jane could feel herself getting upset. She had thought that Jack would be sympathetic and that maybe they could talk things through. "What happened to you Jack? Please tell me?" Jane squeezed his hands.

"I just can't," Jack said softly, almost to himself. "I love you Jane. Don't ever forget that," he said, and pulled away, leaving Jane grasping for his hands, then he turned, walked through his front door and closed it behind him.

Jane was alone in the street, her hands still resting on the wall. She felt tears watering her eyes and distorting her vision. She blinked them out and wiped them away. She felt like banging on the front door and trying to talk things through with Jack, but she knew this wasn't the right time.

Maybe tomorrow, she thought. I'll email him tonight and see him tomorrow. Maybe we can try to have that coffee again. Jane looked up at the windows of Jack's house, trying to catch a glimpse of him, but he wasn't there, so she turned and headed home.

Chapter 14

It was evening when Alfred's stomach told him to finish work and head back to the farmhouse. He had completed repairs to two sides of the perimeter fence and figured he had about three days of work left on fence repairs. It had been tiring, working out at the fringes of the farm away from shade and water, but the solitude had been calming and refreshing, and the repetitive work had allowed him to ponder on his future.

He glanced up at the sun. It was still high, so he guessed it was probably about six o'clock. Not too early to have dinner followed by a hot bath. After all, Fat Joe had told him earlier the council were visiting tomorrow so Alfred suspected he would have a little extra time to himself tonight. It was unlikely that Fat Joe would hit him in the face too—so that was good as well. Confidence and anticipation of the relaxing night ahead lengthened Alfred's stride, allowing him to speed over the grass as if he hadn't laboured on the farm in the sun all day.

Fifteen minutes later, he picked his way down the garden path and pushed the front door open.

"It's me," he shouted, to let them know. They didn't like surprises.

He took his boots off and went straight into the kitchen. He was only allowed in three rooms: the kitchen, bathroom and his bedroom. He knew better than to venture anywhere else—at least while his foster parents were in the house.

Mildred was in the kitchen. "Wash your hands and face," she instructed, dispensing with the type of courtesies that normal people used—like 'hello, how are you?'

"Yes Mildred." Alfred knew better than to hesitate or do anything other than what he was told.

He used soap and water to scrub under his nails with a brush then cupped water in his hands and splashed it on his face and over his head. It felt fantastically cooling, after a day working outside in the sun. After he had washed himself, he washed the grime off the soap and placed it centrally on the soap dish next to the sink, then he rinsed out the sink, carefully dried his hands on a towel and finally rehung the towel neatly on the towel rail. These were all lessons he had learnt the hard way.

"Are you hungry?" Mildred asked.

Silly question, thought Alfred. "Yes Mildred," he replied, noticing the saucepans boiling on the hob, the starched white apron around Mildred's waist and the smell of meat of some description cooking in the oven.

Mildred's thick forearms flexed as she wiped her hands on a clean tea-towel. She was big framed but lean from years of hard work.

"Sit down then," she told him, briskly.

Alfred pulled out a chair from the large table at one end of the kitchen then sat down. There was only one place laid for dinner at the table; Alfred knew Fat Joe and Mildred would eat later, once Alfred was confined to his room for the night.

He poured himself a glass of water from the jug set in front of him and drank slowly from the glass, despite his thirst. He knew better than to glug, rush or display anything other than perfect table manners. He was in Mildred's world now and had to abide by her rules or feel the weight of her wooden spoon on the back of his hands and legs. Only complete obedience and perfect manners were tolerated here. Alfred filled his glass again and drank steadily, making sure he placed the glass back on the table between sips. He took the opportunity to look around as he enjoyed the water.

As always, the kitchen was immaculate—in stark contrast to the decrepit nature of the farm outside that was falling to ruin under the care of Fat Joe—the inside of the farmhouse was fastidiously cleaned, maintained and organised by Mildred. Everything in the house belonged in its own allotted place and woe betide anyone, including Fat Joe, that put anything where it shouldn't be.

Alfred placed his hands on his knees, to stop himself fidgeting or inadvertently moving the knife and fork, placemat, or salt and pepper from their perfect placement on the table, while Mildred, vigorously stirred something in the saucepan then retrieved some sausages from the oven and placed them carefully on a plate sat next to the hob.

Sausage and mash! Alfred hoped. His twitching nose confirmed what his eyes suspected, and he started to salivate. Mildred brought the plate over and laid it down gently, perfectly central on the placemat, then stood straight and crossed her arms over her bosom. She stared down at Alfred.

"Thank you, Mildred," he said, taking care to look her in the eye as he did. Then he looked straight ahead and closed his own eyes. He paused for a second, waiting for a blow to the head or his exposed knuckles while his eyes were shut, but none came so he started to speak in a clear unwavering voice.

"For what I am about to receive, may the Lord make me truly thankful, Amen."

"Amen," Mildred repeated just after Alfred. "Go on then, get on with it. The council are coming tomorrow, and we don't want you looking like an underfed stray."

"Yes Mildred, thank you." Alfred picked up his knife and fork and started to cut into one of the three carefully laid out sausages that lay on the plate. Next to them, lay a large, sculpted mound of potato mash, topped with a sprig of parsley and drizzled in an onion gravy. The food Mildred served day after day was never anything short of perfect.

Mildred watched Alfred eat for a moment, still standing over him with her arms folded, then she retired to the stove to tinker and tidy. Alfred let out a quiet sigh and relaxed—so far so good. The food was delicious as usual, and so far, he hadn't been hit, which was not usual at all. Either he was getting better at conforming to Mildred's strict requirements, or she was being careful because of the visit tomorrow. Either way, it was good for Alfred.

He ate steadily and allowed himself some sneaky looks around as his stomach slowly filled. The kitchen shone, where it had been endlessly scrubbed and polished, and even the area around the hob, where Mildred still worked, was spotless. All the work surfaces were clear except the draining board next to the over-bubbled sink that undoubtedly contained no dirty dishes. Alfred's breath caught as his gaze froze on the draining board and the 'No1 Dad' mug upturned on it to dry.

He looked away quickly as Mildred moved then looked back straight away when he saw that she wasn't watching him.

In the six months that Alfred had been on the farm, he hadn't seen the mug anywhere except in Fat Joe's hand. He had begun to suspect that Fat Joe's podgy pink fingers were jammed in the handle, and that he couldn't put it down. But there it was, all alone on the draining board, with soap suds slowly tracking down its sides, unprotected, vulnerable— detached from the parasite that forever slurped and lapped at its contents.

Alfred continued to stare and imagined himself grabbing the mug and flinging it across the kitchen or smashing it with the hammer from the tool shed, nailing it to the front door next to the jobs list, or dropping it down the well. Endless playbacks of mug destruction ran through his mind one after the other. He could grind it up and force feed it on toast to Fat Joe or hurl it into the herd of cows for them to trample. He could urinate in it, spit in it, cover the rim in cow dung, bury it, drop it, wash it in the toilet bowl, poison it, paint it, change the '1' to a 't'...

"What are you staring at?"

Alfred jolted back to reality and stuck the sausage, skewered on his fork, into his eye.

"Nuthin'... sorry nothing Mildred, I'm just tired. I wasn't staring at anything. I need to get a good night's sleep before the council visit tomorrow that's all." Alfred saw the large wooden spoon in Mildred's hands and hoped that reminding her of the council meeting might stave off a beating.

"Council... yes," her eyes narrowed. "They won't visit the day after tomorrow though, will they." The threat was hardly disguised at all. '*You are safe tonight Alfred but don't get cocky because you are not safe tomorrow night.*'

"No Mildred." Alfred put the last bit of sausage in his mouth, chewed it and swallowed quickly. "I've finished dinner. It was delicious thank you. The sausages were so tasty, and the mashed potato was really creamy. It was perfect." Alfred had learned the hard way to lavish praise on Mildred's cooking.

"Thank you," Mildred looked genuinely pleased. "I've run your bath, up you go. Your clothes for tomorrow are on your bed."

"Thank you, Mildred." Alfred put his knife and fork together on his plate and carried it to the sink where he dutifully waited for Mildred to take it from him. He daren't put it down on the side himself—only Mildred touched Mildred's kitchen.

"Thank you," Mildred took the plate and dismissed Alfred with a nod of her head at the door. He left the kitchen immediately, without speaking another word.

Chapter 15

Jack sat motionless in his bedroom, staring at the phone that lay in the palm of his hand. The screen went dark, so he swiped his thumb across it for the hundredth time, again revealing Dave's number. His thumb hovered over it momentarily, then swiped the screen down and settled on Ginny's number. He moved his thumb away and waited for the screen to darken; when it did he flashed his thumb over the screen to once again reveal Ginny's number then scrolled up to Dave's.

This could take all night, he thought, torn by his indecision. He had a good idea of what he was going to say, but he couldn't make up his mind who to say it to.

Death appearing in the daylight had shaken him. When Death only appeared in Jack's dreams it had been terrible, especially as his version of Death looked like Jane, but now Death was appearing when he was awake he was shaken to his core. There was nowhere to hide. Death could appear, as Jane, and kill him at any moment—even here in the safety of his own bedroom. But not only had Death appeared to Jack today, he was pretty sure Death had appeared to Dave; and he knew Death had appeared to Jane, therefore he must assume that Death had also appeared to Ginny.

I'll phone Ginny, he decided... and ask her if she saw Death today. Jack scrolled down and let the screen darken again without dialling.

If Ginny had seen Death today and Death had killed her, what will she be thinking? Will she decide to take things into her own hands?

Yes definitely, Jack answered his own question. She was 'Action Ginny,' she was not someone that would sit around thinking; she was someone that would act on instinct and just do whatever she thought of first. She was decisive—certain, indecision never slowed her. She would unquestionably do something. The real question was not if she would act, but when and what would she do?

Would she try to kill one of us? Jack mused. She hated Dave—but he was big and not an easy target. Maybe me then? But she likes me, and I'm still the stronger of the two of us so perhaps not.

Jane then! Jane was the weakest, and easiest to kill... and Jane felt like she owed Ginny her life. Maybe Ginny thought that as well. Maybe she was going to want that debt repaying.

Maybe Ginny would try to kill Jane!

No. No chance. No way. Ginny wouldn't do that to Jane.

Jack refreshed the screen and scrolled up to Dave.

Okay what about Dave? I'm certain he saw Death today and ran from him as fast as he could. So, what would he do about it? That's easy, Jack thought. He'll kill Ginny. No doubt about it. In fact, he might think that Ginny would try to kill him and so try to kill her first. That's it. I know who to phone. Jack refreshed the phone and planted his thumb on the name he had decided to ring.

"Hey," Ginny answered.

"Hey," Jack said softly, "how's it going?" he continued.

"How do you think?"

"I think probably not good if you had a day like mine today..." he paused, but Ginny didn't answer. "So, I got killed by Death three times today in broad daylight... while I was awake..." Jack paused again, hoping Ginny would reveal something. He thought, once again, that Ginny wasn't going to answer, but just as he opened his mouth to continue, she started talking.

"Yeah, me too... and there's something else as well."

"What?" Jack prompted.

"It was Jane."

"What was Jane?" Jack asked hoping that Ginny wasn't going to tell him what he thought she meant. But dread filled him—a cold dark hand squeezed his heart and pain filled his chest. He knew what she was going to say.

"Death was Jane. Death came as a dark mist like it always did, but then Jane came out of the mist and strangled me. Death was Jane—Jane was Death... whichever way around you want to say it."

Jack panicked briefly then squeezed his eyes shut and thought for a moment. He had to be quick, so he dived in. "I know Death is Jane."

"What do you mean you know?"

"My Death has been Jane all along. It's Jane that has been killing me in my dreams every night. That's why I didn't want to talk about it. Especially to Jane. I don't want her to start thinking she has to kill herself to end my nightmares."

"Oh my god Jack. How can you bear that?"

"Ginny, I can't bear it. I never could bear it. It's driving me mad"

Jack thought fast. He had thought Ginny would want to kill Dave; he had phoned her to try and make an alliance, but now maybe she didn't want to kill Dave—maybe now she wanted to kill Jane.

"Maybe Death is warning us Jack. Or, telling us—maybe Death is telling us to kill Jane."

"No surely not," Jack answered. "No that doesn't make sense. Death would just tell us if he wanted us to kill Jane. He tells us the balance is wrong, so if he wanted us to kill Jane then he would just tell us that as well."

The conversation was not going as Jack had hoped. Finding out that Ginny was also being killed by Jane was going to make it difficult to get Ginny to ally with him to try and kill Dave.

"Jack?"

"Yes."

"I really think Death wants us to kill Jane... there's no other reasonable explanation. I'm so sorry Jack... that's what I think... and I don't know what to do about it."

Jack waited, trying to think how he could change Ginny's mind. "What if we team up Ginny?"

"What do you mean?"

"Well, I think if we team up, then maybe together we could take Dave. Your brains—my brawn—we could kill him. We could kill Dave, and then it will be balanced again... and Death will leave us alone."

"Will he though?" Ginny replied. "What if it's balanced only if we kill Jane? What if killing Dave has no effect? Who are you going to kill next? Me?"

"No of course not Ginny."

"You answered that a bit quick Jack."

"I just think that you and I could sort this. We don't need to involve Jane. And you hate Dave... I know you do. Let's kill him, and maybe Death will leave us alone...it's worth a shot Ginny... isn't it?" Jack paused waiting for Ginny to reply.

"Ginny?" he prompted and adjusted the phone on his ear. He heard a chair fall backwards then Ginny's phone fall on the floor. There was silence for a moment then more banging that moved away from Ginny's phone—frantic banging, the noise a fight made.

"Ginny!" Jack raised his voice in alarm.

"Jack." The reply came from inside Jack's head. It was his inner voice: the one he used when he was thinking. Jack froze. On the phone he could hear Ginny choking, but also, from just behind him, the floorboards creaked as someone shifted their weight.

"Jack." The voice in his head insisted he acknowledge the presence behind him. While the sound of a struggle continued over the phone, Jack put the phone down and

87

slowly turned to look. Jane stood in the middle of the room. She had the massive scythe in her right hand, the haft resting on the floor and the vicious, curved blade, curling from above her head and down to her feet.

It was Jane's eyes that drew Jack's attention. They were lifeless. They were dead. They weren't really looking at him, instead, they were looking just over him, to where his head would be if he was standing. It was as if the eyes were unused and some other sense was fixing Jack's position.

"I'm going to kill you Jack," the voice in Jack's head said. Jane's lips didn't move.

"Why... why me? And why are you Jane?" Jack felt his mouth dry out and his throat constrict. He thought he wouldn't be able to speak again—he knew what was coming and looked fearfully at the black curved blade with its sharp silver cutting edge. He swallowed the lump in his throat. Perhaps if he kept talking he could put off the inevitable. "What do you want?"

Jane smiled. It was forced, as if an invisible hand had just turned up the sides of her mouth. The smile didn't touch her eyes at all, though. They remained lifeless and fixed just above Jack's head, unseeing and all-seeing at the same time—Jack could never find somewhere to hide from those eyes. They would always find him.

"The balance must be restored." The voice in Jack's head invaded his thoughts again. He tried to push the voice away, but it was his own voice—it was part of him and couldn't be separated from his own thoughts. Jack's head thumped at the effort, but he could still feel Death's presence in his mind. It took over and removed his free will—his capacity to think and to act. He was helpless in the presence of Death. There was nothing he could do.

"The balance must be restored." Jane twisted the haft of the scythe, so that the blade swung towards Jack and the point curved down, inches from his face.

Jack gritted his teeth and looked at the sharp, shiny point of the blade—hovering, motionless just inches from his eyes.

"The balance must be restored," the voice in Jack's head said again. Jack tensed, as Jane viciously thrust her right arm forward, tilting the blade of the scythe and spearing it into Jack's forehead.

"The balance must be restored," his inner voice told him again.

Jack sunk into darkness and felt its cold comfort. He felt the relief a drowning man felt when the struggle for life ended and water filled his lungs. He felt the silence of deafness after an explosion, the numbness after fire had flayed his flesh and burnt away his nerves, and the violent sudden release from the terror of a long fall. Jack sunk into the tranquillity of his own death and bathed in its calmness... anything was better than being tortured by Jane in the guise of Death.

"Jack!" a voice said urgently from somewhere far away.

"Jack!" again.

"Jack!" it persisted.

Jack opened his eyes. He was lying on his front on the blue carpet that lined his bedroom floor, the roughness of the weave against his cheek.

"Jack!" the tiny voice said again.

Jack raised himself and looked around. He grabbed the phone that lay next to him and put it to his ear.

"Hello," he replied hoarsely. His throat felt like it had been sandpapered.

"Oh my God, Jack. Jane strangled me again," Ginny said. "I felt her crush my neck. And my lungs burned as my air ran out. All the time she kept saying, 'the balance must be restored.' What are we going to do?"

Jack tried to gather his thoughts while he looked around fearfully to make sure that Jane had gone.

"Jack... it's not Dave that we need to kill."

Those words terrified Jack and he realised he was going to be unable to convince Ginny that they should kill Dave. He needed to think of something else. He needed time to work it out and he needed to distract Dave and Ginny from turning on Jane. How could he buy time?

"We need to meet. All of us. You, me and Dave, and we need to decide what to do."

"What do you mean Jack?"

"You know what I mean. I'll call Dave and get him onside. Don't tell Jane. It's got to be soon though, before Dave goes ahead and does something himself."

"Okay," Ginny agreed. "Let me know when and where. I'll be there."

"Okay. I'll call you back."

Jack hung up, his mind racing. Maybe I've bought some time, he thought, and scrolled down his phone to call Dave.

Chapter 16

Dave didn't go home like the others, instead, he stalked the streets until dusk set in. As he walked, long shadows merged together to carpet the ground in darkness, while above, branches in the trees became indistinct in the gloom and birds quietened as they roosted. The noise of distant traffic receded as the town settled in for the night and the streets emptied and became devoid of life. Dave didn't settle though.

Anger kept him moving. He was angry that he was being haunted by Death. Angry that he couldn't sleep at night and angry that Death could now find him in daylight. His anger had driven him to decide what to do. He had decided to kill Ginny. He had made up his mind earlier in the graveyard when the four of them had sat together. And the decision was reinforced later when Death killed him in broad daylight.

For months, Death had been torturing him every night in his dreams and now it seemed also in the day. Death had told him the balance was wrong and that someone needed to die. Dave knew who that person should be. Ginny had been brought back from the dead, so now she should go back to being dead. It was straight forward. Easy. Simple. And Dave was going to do it... besides, Jack was too strong, and Jane was under Jack's protection, so Ginny was the easiest target.

After the others had left the graveyard earlier that day, Dave had laid back on the grass and watched the few distant wisps of cloud that slowly drifted by in the blue sky. He had tried to pick up their movement, but they drifted so slowly the movement was imperceptible. That made him angry as well. He flexed his muscles, wanting to use his strength to fight the anger and make it go away, but that was impossible. He needed to focus his strength elsewhere.

His anger had fuelled his thoughts, turning them dark and violent. He had imagined beating Ginny to a pulp with his bare hands—he could just hit her again and again. And then it would be done and then maybe Death would leave him alone.

The last six months had been terrible for Dave. He knew that he had betrayed Jack and Ginny back in January and that they had every right to be angry at him, but he had only been helping Alfred and the spiders to save his dad. He had been put in an impossible position of having to decide who he should try to save and who he should sacrifice.

Anyone else would have done the same thing, he thought. *Ginny would have done the same thing!* Dave was sure of it. And yet for six months she had vented her anger on him. *It wasn't fair!*

Jack mostly just ignored him, but then they hadn't really been friends before... so that was okay. Jane was the worst though. Dave had tried to protect Jane back in January. She knew that, but now she looked at him like she felt sorry for him and for Dave that was worse than being hated.

He loved Jane—he always had—but her pity was unbearable. Her pity tortured him, it damaged and confused him, it ate up his humanity and stoked up his anger. The pressure was unbearable, so he had to release the pain before he exploded. He had to vent.

I'm going to kill Ginny, he had decided, and if that doesn't work, I'll find a way to kill Jack, and if that doesn't work I'll kill Jane. I've got to stop the pain, stop the dreams, stop Death. Stuff them. I'll kill them all, and I'll keep on killing until Death leaves me alone.

It was then, as Dave had lounged on the grass in the graveyard that afternoon that Death had killed him again, but it was daylight and he was awake.

Dave shuddered at the memory. That had been earlier. Now it was dusk, and he had walked all afternoon and evening. He was thirsty now and his feet ached, but the anger still raged inside him.

I'm gonna kill Ginny—I'm gonna kill Ginny—I'm gonna kill Ginny. He sang it in his head, first putting the words to tunes from current songs, then some nursery rhymes, and finally settling for a Christmas carol. *I'm gonna kill Ginny— I'm gonna kill Ginny—I'm gonna kill Ginny all the way.*

He laughed out loud; an amused laugh, the sort of laugh delivered in response to a funny joke, not a malevolent laugh. And in that laugh, he sensed the depth of his despair and just how deep he had plunged into madness—singing about killing Ginny was funny!

That set him off laughing again and he launched his mirth out into the night. His laugh split the quiet and the trees lining the road rustled in applause. The rustling grew louder in his ears as he laughed, and just too late he realised that it wasn't the leaves rustling in applause to his singing, that he could hear—it was Death.

Dave span round just as Death descended through a gap in the tree canopy. He reacted and put his hands up in defence, but it was too late. Death was upon him. Dave looked up and took in the small details rather than the whole terrible image in front of him: the one broken talon on the outstretched, clawed foot; the black, shredded cloak that streamed out from behind the creature; the wide, black wings on which black veins branched out and pulsed; the muscled arms that ended in sharp, hooked claws that reached out for him; the manacled wrists from which broken chains hung; and Jane's twisted face, screaming in fury.

The clawed hands and feet hit Dave simultaneously; he blacked out for a moment then came-to as Death's wings beat furiously and lifted him from the ground. He cried out in pain as the claws and talons penetrated deep into his flesh and found gaps between his ribs. The noise from the wings beat like a giant bass drum as the creature gained height. Dave bounced in rhythm to the beating of the wings, his flesh stretching and tearing with each beat, separating from bone and sinew. He screamed.

Pain opened his eyes and he stared into Jane's face just inches from his own. Her foul breath, hot on his cheek was rancid, putrid. He gagged and choked. Jane smiled and retracted her claws from his body. Dave screamed again with the last of his breath as he plummeted back through the trees and smashed onto the tarmac road below.

He woke in an instant, flat on his back in the road, arms and legs spread-eagled. His phone buzzed in his pocket, so he reached in and grabbed it without getting up.

"Yep?" he answered, still on his back looking up at the stars through the trees.

"Dave it's Jack. We need to talk."

"Again? We talked this afternoon."

"Yeah, I know but things are different now."

"Is that so."

"Yeah... erm... listen. Have you seen Death at all today? Because Ginny and I have both been killed during the daylight today. It doesn't matter whether we're asleep or awake anymore, Death can kill us wherever, whenever."

"Yep. Hang on." Dave rolled onto his front, got his knees under him and pushed himself up. "I was laying in the road, just thought I had better get up."

"The road?"

"Yep. Death dropped me there."

"Ah... okay. So, Death is getting you as well."

"Yep."

"So, the other bit of news is that Death has got Jane's face now... and... ehm... that probably means something. I didn't tell you before, but my version of Death has had Jane's face since the start. It's always been Jane that's been killing me, but now its Jane that's killing Ginny as well."

"Yep."

"I think we need to meet again. But this time without Jane."

"Without Jane? Now that's interesting."

"Ehm, Ginny agrees, so if you agree as well then perhaps tomorrow morning?"

"Yep. Meet at the church again. We can use one of the Sunday school rooms inside. I'll get the key off the vicar."

"Okay. I'll phone Ginny and let her know, then text you the time."

"Yep." Dave said and hung up.

Hmmm, he thought to himself. I'm gonna need a new song.

"I'm gonna kill Jane—I'm gonna kill Jane—I'm gonna kill Jane all the way."

Chapter 17

Alfred laid in bed, staring at the white-washed ceiling as it changed hue from orange to red then dimmed to darkness. He kept his mind awake by imagining patterns in the stippled ceiling until the dark hid it from him. Then, in his mind's eye, he counted spiders in lieu of sheep jumping over a fence. Giant, fearsome spiders that would do as he directed and fill Fat Joe with so much poison that he would split open and it would leak out like a burst abscess.

He imagined arriving in Middle Gratestone at the head of a spider army, seeking out Jane, Jack and Ginny. One by one, his spiders would strip tiny pieces of flesh from their bones and devour it, tiny piece by tiny piece, until only skeletons were left.

"Have you locked the door?" Mildred's voice, speaking to Fat Joe and her footsteps coming up the stairs. Alfred focused and listened, imagining their movements.

"Yes dear." Fat Joe's voice. Further away, downstairs somewhere. Mildred's footsteps crossing the landing and moving away to the room she shared with Fat Joe. A door opening. Footsteps coming up the stairs, then on the landing moving away and the bedroom door closing, the voices now muffled and indistinct.

Alfred let out the breath that he had been holding, in a long slow sigh and waited patiently for Fat Joe and Mildred to settle. Twenty minutes later, Alfred could hear Fat Joe's rasping snore—even thirty feet distant and two closed doors hadn't fully muffled the racket. Alfred pulled back his covers and placed his bare feet on the floorboards causing the springs in his bed to squeak lightly so he waited and listened before standing.

Five silent steps later, he was at the door of his bedroom. He looked back around his room; he could clearly see a lighter square through the curtain that covered the window on the far wall and the dark patch of the wardrobe at the bottom of his bed. So far so good, he thought. There should be sufficient light for him to see his way.

Alfred slowly turned the door handle and eased the bedroom door open. Moonlight from a window stretched the full length of the landing and picked out the reading desk and chaise longue that were the only items of furniture here. Alfred looked left and right then stepped out and softly closed the door.

The bathroom door was open, but the furthest corners were lost in the dark of the windowless room. Alfred stepped in and felt carefully along the shelving unit for Mildred's hairbrush. His fingertips found something akin to a hairy hedgehog, so he gently lifted it off the shelf and headed for the stairs.

Fat Joe's snoring increased in volume as Alfred closed the distance between himself and the source of the noise then decreased in volume as he descended the stairs into pitch blackness. There were no windows in the hall, so he trusted his memory and shuffled forward, feeling with his bare feet for any obstructions on the floor, then reaching out for the door in front of him. He touched panelled wood then quickly found the door handle and slowly twisted it open.

The kitchen had windows on three sides and seemed almost bright after the darkness of the hallway. Alfred crossed to the draining board and sink, and immediately saw that Fat Joe's 'No1 Dad' mug was gone, so starting from the draining board and moving outwards, he began opening cupboards.

Two cupboards down on the left, he found a shelf full of mugs, right at the front was the 'No1 Dad' mug. Alfred reached out and took his prize. He twisted it up and around triumphantly, inspecting it reverently from all angles.

This is going to be fun, he thought, and set to work.

First, he held the hairbrush up in the moonlight and selected the longest strand of Mildred's hair that he could find and tugged it gently free from the hairbrush's grip. Then he fed it through the mug handle four times and pulled it tight, barely suppressing a giggle as he did so.

With satisfied smugness, Alfred placed the mug back on the shelf in the cupboard and closed the cupboard door while still holding onto the strand of hair; then he looped the strand four times around the cupboard door handle and stepped back.

Alfred smiled, then regained control, then grinned. He tried to calm himself, but his grin got wider then his stomach cramped causing him to bend over to stifle the hysterical laughter that was threatening to burst out of him and give him away. His knees collapsed, and he fell to the floor as he struggled to breathe between silent sobs of laughter.

After five minutes, that felt like five hours, Alfred regained control and slunk back to his room. He was really looking forward to tomorrow...

Chapter 18

"I'm gonna kill Jane—I'm gonna kill Jane—I'm gonna kill Jane all the way. Hmm hmm hm hmm—hmm hmm hm hmm—hmm hmm hm hmm hmm hm hmm."

"Wait!" Dave stopped humming in the middle of the road. A lightbulb came on in his head. He looked left, right, behind then ahead. He had been walking aimlessly with no idea of direction or plan of reaching any destination. The lightbulb in his head required that he found out where he was.

"School Road, two hundred yards from Café Shack, Church Road is first right then first left, Jane's house is one quarter of a mile beyond the church," he reported the information to himself. Then turned his attention to the lightbulb that was flashing brightly in his mind and the questions that it was asking.

Why wait for the others? Why wait until morning? Why not just go to Jane's house now and kill her? Why not…?

He stood stock still in the middle of the road and looked inward into the dark depths of his own mind. His reality was different now. He no longer cared about people and what they were doing. He no longer cared what they thought and what they might think of him. If a car drove up the road now he would scarcely noticed. The car would have had to go around him because he would not move—not until he had thought this through. Not until he had answers to the questions flashing in his mind.

Kill Jane now, or kill Jane tomorrow? Why wait until tomorrow? If I kill her now, maybe I can sleep tonight without fear of being killed by Death. If I wait until tomorrow, Death could kill me again and again. I need sleep. I'll do anything to get some sleep. Kill Jane now then. Get it over with. Get it done. Then sleep.

Dave put one foot in front of the other, froze for a second, then started walking in the direction of Jane's house.

Tonight. I'm going to kill Jane, tonight, he decided.

He looked around the road. Not for people. Not for witnesses that might tell the police investigating Jane's murder that they had seen him. People were unimportant. He looked around for Death, but there was no sign. He passed the Café Shack, but it was closed, and the lights were off, so he turned right, passed under the giant oak tree near the school then reached the top of Church Road.

He stopped here and looked down the entire length of the road. The church was shrouded in darkness and only the outline of the tower was clear, silhouetted against the starry sky. The cottages were similarly dark, except for one that provided an oasis of light about halfway down the road. Everywhere was silent. There were no birds, no movement and no wind. Dave set off straight for the oasis, lured by the illusion of safety that it might provide. As he walked he started to think about how he might kill Jane.

Okay, he thought. Jane's probably in bed asleep, or more likely in bed too scared to sleep. So, should I try to get her to come outside somehow, or try to get inside? Her parents were likely at home so that meant the front door was out of the question. They might stop him or call the police then the police would stop him. Jail didn't matter if he killed Jane before he was caught. But being caught before he killed her? That would be a disaster. Death could kill him every night in his prison cell and he wouldn't be able to do a thing about it. The back door then, or her bedroom window? I'll go around the back, Dave decided.

He knew which window was the one to Jane's bedroom. She had lived in the same house for years and he had visited there on-and-off since he was a boy. Her house backed onto fields, so he could access the house from the back and then either get in through the backdoor or climb up to Jane's bedroom window.

Dave reached the oasis and strode into its golden glow. It lent him a blanket of comfort for a moment and his mood briefly lifted, but all too soon he reached the other side and again stepped into darkness. His thoughts returned to the task at hand. Dark thoughts, in the dark of night—they fitted well.

How do I kill Jane? he questioned. It's got to be quiet or her parents will hear and try to stop me and call the police—I can't take them all on. So, if it's got to be quiet, then it needs to be quick before she can struggle. Quick and quiet—yeah quick and quiet. Dave nodded, agreeing with his own logic.

The uncertainty fell away from his stride and he stretched his legs to eat up the distance. The road was dark between the hedges that lined the last few hundred yards to Jane's house, so he kept his eye on the top of the hedge to keep himself in the centre of the road and kept walking hard until he was alongside the field behind Jane's house. He spotted the lesser darkness of a gap in the hedge and found the five-bar gate that led into the field. It was secured by a latch on the gatepost and felt sturdy, so he climbed over.

The field was mostly used for grazing cattle; the cows were probably in a corner somewhere settling in for the night. The grass was tufted and uneven, so he slowed and took care in the dark. The ground rose steadily in front of him to the crest of the hill, behind which, Jane's house was nestled in a hamlet of four houses. The lights from the houses were not yet in view so he picked out the Great Bear constellation, used it to find the North Star and used that to head in the direction he thought would lead to the back of Jane's house.

"Quick and quiet," he said to himself as he made steady progress in the dark. Anticipation was causing his nerves to become taut, like overtightened wire they waited to snap at the slightest touch. Adrenalin pumped around his body and his heartrate rose. The slow pace at which he was having to walk in the field did nothing to release the energy building up inside him. He was breathing quickly and lightly and felt the first tremors in his hands that revealed his anxiousness.

"MESSAGE FROM THE DARK SIDE YOU HAVE!" His phone shrilled in his pocket.

"Jesus!" Dave jumped and reached for his phone. The screen shone out like a lighthouse beam in the night. He set the phone ringtone to silent then read the message.

'10AM at the church.' It was from Jack.

'Yep,' Dave tapped in, sent his reply then pocketed his phone.

"Jesus," he said again, and looked around. His night vision had been destroyed by looking at his phone and now the inky darkness, underneath the starry sky above, swallowed up the hillside around him. He looked up to check the North Star and set his direction once again. The crest of the hill where it met the night sky didn't seem so far away now, so he took one step forward then froze...

Slow steady breathing pulsed in the air ahead. He couldn't see any shape or form in the dark, but he could sense the presence of something in front of him. His breath caught, then choked off midway as his throat constricted in fear and his mouth dried out.

"Get on with it then," Dave said through gritted teeth, in anticipation of Death appearing from out of the dark. His voice was strained, and his throat hurt as he forced the words through the lump that had lodged there.

The presence up ahead moved and snorted loudly in response to his words. Dave hesitated for a moment then stepped forward.

A snort and a stamp.

Dave raised his hands in front of him and walked into the solid side of a cow. It mooed loudly and swung its head knocking into him, forcing him to stumble backwards. Other cows mooed in response and slowly the herd started to move towards and around him in the dark, circling him. Another cow came in from the side at a canter and hit him a hard but glancing blow; had it been full on, it would have crushed him. Dave reeled away from the impact and realised the real physical danger that he was in, he could easily get trampled by the angry herd, and become the 'plus-one' that Death required.

Angry snorts and stamps of hard hooves filled the darkness with noise. Dave backed up a few steps then half-remembered something.

Didn't cows only run uphill and downhill or something, and not along the side of a hill? It made sense he decided and so he turned and ran along the contour of the hill away from the herd, heading towards the side of the field that paralleled the lane to Jane's house. He could hear the hooves hammering on the ground behind him and the cows mooing angrily.

Goddammit, maybe they could run along a hillside, he thought.

He increased his pace; the hooves sounded like thunder now. The hedge that lined the lane must be up ahead he thought and tried to gauge the distance, perhaps one-hundred-yards he guessed. Okay I'll do a countdown.

"Ten-nine-eight-seven-six-five-four—Jesus!" he exclaimed in pain as he ran straight into the tall hedge. His hands took the brunt of the impact, but his momentum carried him into the tangled mass, where branches stabbed at him and something sharp lanced along his temple and opened a long cut. He pulled his arms away, leaving skin hanging from thorns and barbs then took a step back.

The hooves were closing, so he dropped to his hands and knees and powered himself headlong into the hedge at ground level. He ducked his head, but the hedge tore at him as he burrowed forwards. The cows smashed into the hedge around him and lowed in pain and alarm. The noise echoed around the hillside and spurred Dave on, spikes and snags grabbing at his hair and clothes, and ripping his skin, until finally he dropped through onto the lane that led to Jane's house.

Doors in the hamlet up the road were opening, spilling light and people into the lane.

"What's got into 'em?"

"Something's spooked them."

"I've got a flashlight, hang on"

A torch flashed on and started lighting up the hedge line, it moved down the lane searching the darkness.

Dave turned and ran away, torn and bloodied. As he rounded the corner back onto Church Road and slowed his pace in relief, he heard the beating of wings approaching from behind him. He could see the oasis of light up ahead

that had comforted him earlier, so he stretched out his legs
and ran hard, but never made it....

Chapter 19

The knock on the front door woke Alfred, Fat Joe and Mildred all at the same time. And, at the same time, they all remembered the visit from the council. Alfred leapt to his feet and tugged on the clothes that Mildred had laid out for him on his bed last night: dark chinos, light chequered shirt and dark socks. She had laid them out from top to bottom as if the invisible man had been steamrolled on the bed. Alfred had dumped them on the floor last night before getting into bed and retrieved them from there now.

Fat Joe was cursing loudly, and Mildred was scolding everyone and everything as they both pulled on their own clothes in a panic. Alfred was first out onto the landing.

"Get the door," Fat Joe snapped as he rushed by to the toilet in vest and unbuttoned trousers. Alfred paused until he could hear Fat Joe relieving himself then slowly plodded down the stairs; he was in no rush.

The knock sounded again, louder this time. Alfred continued his slow descent. He could hear Mildred still scolding herself in the bedroom, and Fat Joe finishing off in the toilet in ever weaker spurts and a long fart.

A third knock reverberated around the hall. Alfred pulled back the deadbolts, turned the key in the lock and pulled the front door open. A man he recognised but couldn't name stood at the threshold.

"Good morning Alfred," the man in the grey wrinkled suit said. He smiled an overly happy sort of smile, too happy for this early on a Sunday morning. "Are they employing you as a doorman now?" he guffawed loudly at his own weak joke. Alfred didn't join in.

"No," he replied and decided to wear his blank face to see what happened.

The man in the suit smiled. "Will you be going to church today?" he asked.

"Spec so," replied Alfred, not that Fat Joe and Mildred had ever taken him before.

"Jolly good. Now, could you inform your foster parents that Mr Bar... aha! Here they are."

Alfred glanced back to see that Fat Joe and Mildred had made it to the foot of the stairs. "Mr Bar-aha is here," he informed them.

"Good morning Mr Barrington," Fat Joe and Mildred replied together in harmony.

"Come in, come in, Mr Barrington. Don't stand on ceremony." Mildred waved Mr Barrington in. "We can sit at the kitchen table and have a nice chat. I'll put the kettle on. Tea or coffee, Mr Barrington?"

"Oh, tea of course thank you Mildred. Milk, no sugar please."

"Certainly Mr Barrington. Through you go Joe. Alfred come on stop dawdling, into the kitchen with you."

Mr Barrington followed Alfred, who followed Fat Joe, into the kitchen. Mildred shut the front door and followed them all.

"Oh!" she exclaimed as soon as she walked into the kitchen.

Alfred was already following Fat Joe to the table, so he looked back at Mildred as she stalked across the kitchen, picked up her hairbrush and held it aloft.

"My hairbrush," she stated and turned to Alfred, who she saw pick up his jaw that had dropped in surprise then quickly look away and sit at the table. He then studiously looked down.

"Pull out Mr Barrington's chair please Alfred," she said calmly, still holding the hairbrush up in the air as she also noted Joe's expression. Clearly, he had no idea why the hairbrush was there.

Alfred jumped up, pulled out Mr Barrington's chair then sat back down again, his sense of unease growing with every passing second. Would Mildred put two-and-two together and connect the hairbrush and Fat Joe's mug to him? Should he tell Mildred now about the mug before it got broke? What would they do if they knew that it was him that had boobytrapped the mug?

No, stuff them both... I hate them... this will be the best thing that's ever happened here... stuff them both... I'm evil reborn. I will have my revenge on them and on everyone else... stuff 'em. And stuff that mug... I hope it smashes... I hope he cries....

I'm gonna kill them anyway.

Alfred made up his mind; his plot was running now anyway, and he would live with whatever happened.

"Thank you, Alfred," Mr Barrington said as he sat down. So, how are you enjoying the country air out here?" he asked.

"Er—"

"Did you enjoy the eggs Mr Barrington?" Fat Joe interrupted Alfred's answer.

"Oh yes thank you Joe that was very nice of you."

"No problem, anytime."

"So yes, where was I? Alfred are you happy here?" Mr Barrington asked.

"I—"

"And the milk I dropped off yesterday. Fresh as you can get that was. Makes a lovely cup of tea... did you like it?"

"Yes, yes and so did Mrs Barrington, thank you Joe."

"You're very welcome," said Fat Joe.

"So, Alfred—"

"I'll drop some bread off tomorrow, about ten in the morning. Mildred is getting up early to bake a fresh batch, so it will be delicious. Maybe with jam for late breakfast or early lunch, whichever you prefer."

They all looked at Mildred as she filled the kettle with water.

"Oh, thank you Mildred for going to all that trouble to bake for me—"

113

"No trouble at all Mr Barrington," replied Mildred, and flashed a smile at him. "You know how much we enjoy supporting your work as a councillor, and if I can do anything on top of the money that we donate every month then that's no trouble either. Isn't that right Joe?" Mildred said as she opened the cupboard to retrieve the mugs.

"Yes, that's right Mildre—BLOODY HELL!" Fat Joe exclaimed as his 'No1 Dad' mug jumped out of the cupboard, glanced off the edge of the kitchen worksurface and exploded on the hard slate-tiled floor.

Fat Joe jumped to his feet before the last piece of broken mug stopped skittering across the floor. He stared, mouth agape, at his favourite mug scattered far and wide about the kitchen.

Mildred's look of shock quickly disappeared as her sharp eyes found Alfred's and bored into him. Her jaw muscles tightened, and her head twitched to one side; she clenched and unclenched her hands on the tea towel that she held, wringing it in silent fury. She didn't know how it had been done, but she was certain that Alfred was the culprit.

"Oh dear," said Alfred.

Fat Joe's eyes snapped away from the pieces of his mug and he too stared at Alfred.

"How did you do that Mildred?" Alfred asked.

Mildred's mouth opened twice to speak, and closed again without uttering one word, then she managed a weak smile that looked like a dog showing its teeth.

"Oh," she managed then collected herself. "No one move," she instructed. "I'll get a broom and clean this up. It's only a mug."

"..." Fat Joe whimpered.

"Yes, of course Mildred. Accidents happen," said Mr Barrington. "Darnedest thing though, it seemed to jump right off the shelf."

"Didn't it just," agreed Mildred, not looking up from the soft broom that she was gliding around the room to collect up the remains of Fat Joe's mug. "Tea will be right up though, Mr Barrington. Would you like some biscuits with it?"

"Oh yes. Delightful thank you Mildred. Alfred, you are very lucky to have such generous foster parents looking after you. I can see that you are being well looked after here."

"I know," replied Alfred, then turned to look at Fat Joe. "Was that your mug?" he asked—deadpan. "It looked like your mug—hard to tell now though. Was it yours?" Alfred asked his questions in an as concerned tone as he could manage. "It looked like your number one dad mug, yes there's half of a '1' there. The top half I think. Can you see it Joe?" Alfred asked and pointed to the piece on the floor as Mildred hurriedly tried to sweep up the last remnants into a dustpan.

Alfred continued, "I'm lucky I don't have anything really. That means I have nothing to lose... nothing to get upset about."

"Oh, I'm sure that's not true Alfred, and if it is for now then it won't be for always." Mr Barrington looked kindly at Alfred. "So, how's school? The headmaster tells me you have a firm grasp of English, Maths and History, but not so good at the sciences."

"I like school, thank you Mr Barrington. I wish I could go every day."

"Ha-ha, that's the spirit Alfred," laughed Mr Barrington. "You've got a real scholar here Joe."

"Yes, we're very lucky," Joe said through gritted teeth. He had evidently caught up with Mildred and realised that Alfred had had something to do with the demise of his mug.

"Here you go, Mr Barrington," Mildred placed a mug of steaming tea in front of him. "Alfred dear," she placed a mug in front of Alfred then walked back to get the two mugs she had left on the side. "Joe," she said as she placed a mug in front of Fat Joe then slid onto the chair next to him.

Fat Joe stared at the little pony with a rainbow coloured tail and mane, on the side of the mug. His lip curled up in distaste and his eyes swam with sadness at the loss that he had suffered. Tea would not taste the same from this mug. Gently he picked it up and blew softly across the top, then sipped carefully as if it was poison.

Mr Barrington flicked his eyes between Fat Joe and Alfred, between distaste and innocence.

"Help yourself to the biscuits," Mildred pushed the plate across the table towards Mr Barrington.

"Thank you, don't mind if I do."

"So, are we going to have the delight of Alfred staying with us a little longer?"

"Well yes, I think so Mildred. Alfred is obviously happy here, I can see that you are taking great care of him. And Alfred..." Mr Barrington looked at Alfred. "We shall try to find you an adoptive family, but I'm sorry to say that you are a little old for adoption."

Alfred shrugged and took a biscuit from the plate; at one-hundred-and-thirteen-years-old, he probably was a little too old for adoption. He saw Mildred watching him. He could tell she resented every biscuit he had, that she resented the cup of tea she had made him, and she was desperate to end this charade and punish him for breaking Fat Joe's mug. Her eyes narrowed as Alfred bit into the biscuit and crumbs dropped onto her perfect kitchen table.

"Mmm, these are good," Alfred said, waving the biscuit in front of her. Determined to make the most of his temporary safety.

"Aren't they just," agreed Mr Barrington.

"Well we would be delighted to keep Alfred here Mr Barrington... I'm sure we can find plenty for him to do. Isn't that right Joe?"

"Yeah. Plenty."

Alfred looked at Fat Joe; the pretence of being nice, seemed to be taking its toll on him. Fat Joe looked grim and the forced kindness was draining from his voice.

"Well that is good. I must say I couldn't be happier, and I shall ensure that Alfred remains here for as long as necessary. Thank you, Joe, Mildred... and for the hospitality of course."

"Always a pleasure, Mr Barrington. Isn't that so Joe?"

"Always." Fat Joe was just staring at Alfred now, almost all his pretence had gone.

"Well I think I have taken enough of your time. I must be off."

"We'll see you out Mr Barrington and Joe will be round tomorrow with the bread... won't you Joe."

"'Course." Fat Joe was still staring at Alfred, boring holes into him with his eyes.

"I'll come out Mr Barrington," Alfred said.

"And us... come on Joe," Mildred jumped to her feet in an obvious attempt to stop Alfred from having a chance to speak to Mr Barrington on his own.

They all trooped outside, down the path and into the courtyard where a silver-grey car was parked. Alfred liked the rounded lines of modern cars and eyed it appreciatively. He was fascinated by all cars and spent as much time as he could on the toilet reading Fat Joe's car magazines that were stored there.

Mr Barrington jumped in and put the driver's window down.

"Cheerio folks," he waved a hand, which Fat Joe, Mildred and Alfred all returned, then he pulled away.

Alfred started to count; he figured he had about fifteen to twenty seconds before the car pulled out of the courtyard, passed around the garages and headed out of sight. Twenty seconds before pain. Twenty seconds before Fat Joe and Mildred exploded. Twenty seconds before they punished him for the destruction of the mug.

Alfred smiled—whatever happened it had been worth it. "That new mug suits you Joe," Alfred laughed. He was giddy with nervous tension. He could feel it coming... any second... any second. Mr Barrington's car disappeared around the corner.

CRACK!

Alfred didn't know who hit him, or what he was hit with, but something hit him hard on the back of the head. There was a bright, white flash behind his eyes and he was flung forward towards the cobblestones. He tried to break his fall with his hands, but everything went black before he hit the ground.

Chapter 20

It was the cold shock that brought Alfred back to consciousness. He was face down in water and it filled his mouth and nose and forced him awake. He scrabbled around and tried to right himself, but a strong hand gripped the hair on the back of his head and held him under. Alfred grabbed at the wooden bottom and opened his eyes underwater; diffused light came in from above and he realised he was being held underwater in the pig trough.

The hand pulled him out and forcefully turned his head to look at the face of his attacker. Alfred blinked the water out of his eyes and sucked in a lungful of air. Fat Joe's ugly face came into focus.

"Did you think that was funny?" Fat Joe screamed. "Did you think you would get away with it? You little s—" Fat Joe's words were drowned out as he thrust Alfred underwater again.

Only Alfred's head and shoulders were in the trough, his legs and body were outside kneeling in the ground with Fat Joe's bulk pinning him there. Alfred tried to move his legs to kickout, but it was impossible, so he planted his hands on the bottom of the trough to push himself up, but he wasn't strong enough. His hands disturbed the sludge in the trough and it swilled around, so that he tasted the rotten leaves and faecal matter that had built up over the years. It went up his nose, in his eyes and covered him in filth. It was slimy and thick. His hands slipped around in it as he tried to resist, turning the water black, cutting out the light from above.

Fat Joe pulled him out. "I'm going to make you wish you were never born!" He allowed Alfred just enough time to grab a breath then thrust him under again, pushing him all the way down so his face was in the rancid sludge; it squeezed into his mouth as he grimaced and tried to turn away. Fat Joe pressed down hard, crushing Alfred's face against the bottom. Alfred pushed up again but without success. Anger boiled up in him and burst out. It gave him strength. Power returned to his arms, so he was able to push harder. Blood pumped around his body as his heart beat in huge powerful pumps and adrenalin flooded his system.

Fat Joe pulled him out. "Not so cocky now, are you?" he screamed. Alfred coughed out filth and sucked in air, then he was under again. Rage replaced the anger and lit the fire that had lain dormant inside him. Alfred sensed the spiders in the barn and in the eaves of the farmhouse.

Rage! he realised. It was rage that he had been missing. It was rage that he had needed to control the spiders. And now he had it again. Rage boiled inside him. It was an inferno, a maelstrom of fire. Alfred used it to reach out to the creatures around him.

He saw Fat Joe holding him down, through the eyes of the rats in the stables. He took in the panoramic view of the farm from the hawk, high in the sky. He saw multiple visions of himself in the eyes of the spiders dotted around the farmyard. The animals all watched, waiting.

121

Alfred called out to the spiders first. They dropped from their webs and scurried across the ground. They submitted to his rage. They fed on it and were enraptured by it. They worshipped it and did what Alfred commanded but they were too far away. Alfred's lungs burned, and his vision darkened. Sparks went off behind his eyes while his ears echoed with the furious beating of his heart.

Fat Joe pulled him out. "Have you had enough?" he screamed.

A piercing screech ripped through the air and Fat Joe screamed again as the hawk's talons raked his scalp. Alfred snapped his head back and headbutted Fat Joe in the face then elbowed him in the stomach. Fat Joe staggered back. Alfred pulled away from him and turned to watch. The hawk beat the air around Fat Joe, ripped at his skin and pecked his hands as he tried to fend it off. Then it was gone, gaining height to rise away, to be Alfred's eyes once more.

Alfred and Fat Joe stood facing each other. Fat Joe touched tentatively at his head and searched the sky for the hawk. Alfred stood in place and slowly raised his arms until he was in the shape of a cruciform. He closed his eyes and looked through the eyes of the hundreds of creatures that approached.

Fat Joe wiped blood from his forehead with the back of his hand. It glistened there as he clenched and unclenched his fingers. He looked surprised and stupid with his hair sticking up in tatty blooded lumps atop his scalp. Alfred smiled as he continued to watch through hundreds of eyes.

"That was you." Fat Joe accused him. "You did something to that bird... that wasn't natural." There was a wariness in Fat Joe's voice that hadn't been there before. "What did you do?" he asked. "Tell me, or I'll beat it out of you."

The hundreds of eyes started to arrive at Fat Joe's boots. They climbed up and spread out across his clothing, blanketing first his trouser legs then the back of his unbuttoned gilet and across his shirt.

"How did you do it?" Fat Joe brushed at his shoulder as something tickled him.

Alfred opened his eyes and took in the swarm of spiders that scurried across the ground in a river of black. Those that had reached Fat Joe, climbed up to a gap in clothing and paused there, waiting for others to join them.

Fat Joe brushed at his neck. "There's something very wrong with you, and I know just the cure... it's four-foot-long, made of leather and used to whip cows. So help me God, I'm going to draw blood from your back today," he seethed.

"No, you won't." Alfred said, still stood with his arms outstretched.

"Who's going to stop me—you?"

"No, not me." Alfred's smile widened.

"Who then—Barrington? He's too fond of Mildred's cooking. He won't help you."

"No, not Mr Barrington." Alfred giggled, momentarily drunk on the power that surged through him.

Fat Joe took a step forward. In response, Alfred dropped his arms to signal the hundreds of spiders that covered Fat Joes back. They swarmed forward, finding the gaps between Fat Joe's clothes and his flesh. They surged over his shirt collar and down his neck. They squirmed through the gaps between his shirt buttons, shirt cuffs and up his trouser legs. Then, as they found a clear piece of Fat Joe's flesh, they bit down hard and injected their poison into him.

Others followed on behind, they crawled over their brothers and sisters until they too found a clear patch of flesh and added their poison to that already being pumped into Fat Joe's body.

Fat Joe gurgled as if drowning and jerked around like a drunk puppet, arms flailing. His eyes bulged as if they would burst from their sockets, and his mouth opened and closed until the spiders reached it and rushed in. They swarmed over his face and Fat Joe disappeared in a writhing mass that staggered around in circles then dropped to the ground.

Alfred watched happily, his smile twitching in response to Fat Joe's twitching body on the ground. The more twitching—the wider the smile. Then like the end of a Shakespearian tragedy, Fat Joe rose to his knees, held the pose for a moment in encore then collapsed. The spiders continued to writhe over his corpse, their own bodies hiding the destruction that they wrought on Fat Joe's flesh.

Alfred sat back on the wooden edge of the pig trough, in satisfaction.

"I told you that you wouldn't draw blood from my back," he said. "Now you'll never hurt me again."

Chapter 21

Jack arrived at Jane's house. It was early for him to be up and about, but he wanted to see Jane just one more time before the last time that he would ever see her. He had about two hours to wait until he met with the others, but it didn't seem long enough.

He looked around warily. Death in the guise of Jane, had visited him more than once in the night. That wasn't uncommon these days, but what was uncommon, was that his neck still hurt where it had been cut through by Jane's scythe. He wondered whether it was his brain tricking him or whether Death was gaining strength. Perhaps Death would manifest, become solid somehow, and the wounds inflicted would then be real.

Or it's just in my head, he thought.

He touched his fingers to his neck at the memory then checked his fingertips for blood, which thankfully were all clear. He tapped lightly at the door, in case Jane's parents were still asleep—it was Sunday after all. He had emailed Jane earlier and she opened the door immediately with a finger on her lips to indicate he should be quiet.

They tiptoed into the kitchen and shut the door behind them to muffle their conversation. Jane moulded herself into Jack's tall frame until there was no space between them and hugged him tightly for a long moment.

"Hey," she said into his shoulder.

"Hi." Jack nuzzled the top of her head. She was freshly showered, and her hair was still damp. "No eau de fly spray yet," he murmured into her hair.

"I'm saving that for later," Jane's voice was husky.

"I'm sorry I was weirded out yesterday Jane. I know I should be stronger, it just all gets to me sometimes."

"I know. Me too."

"Apology accepted."

"Hey, I wasn't apologising... you big dope." Jane laughed.

"Well it sounded like that to me." Jack smiled.

"Whatever—make yourself useful and put the kettle on."

"What! I'm a guest here."

"Well, when you become a paying guest, instead of a freeloading one, I'll make the tea."

"Fair enough. So, I guess that will be like—never? Shall I do some toast as well?"

"I've already had breakfast thanks."

"Ehm." Jack rubbed his stomach.

"Don't you have a toaster round yours?"

"Well that would have meant staying at mine longer and not seeing you until later. I couldn't bear that."

"Good answer, Jack! Such a charmer." Jane looked at Jack. "It's nice to have a normal conversation, like normal people, instead of... you know."

"Yeah, of course I know. Normal is not something we've had a lot of lately."

"No, it isn't."

"So, I'll ask first then. Did you get killed last night?"

"Of course," Jane lied.

"Me too, five times I think."

"And are you going to tell me what happened?"

Jack shook his head. He would never tell Jane that she was killing him every night in his dreams and that she had killed him on his way to her house that morning. And, that apart from the scythe and the eyes, he couldn't tell Jane apart from Death. Although, he suspected that now Jane was also killing Dave and Ginny that they would tell Jane at the first opportunity. "You know I don't talk about it," he said simply.

Jane nodded and sighed. "It's up to you." She passed two slices of bread to Jack for him to put in the toaster then laid the table out with a plate, knife, jam, butter and a milk jug. Just like normal people, she thought.

The kettle boiled. Jack filled the teapot while Jane laid out the cups and saucers. Normal people doing normal things, she thought again. Nice normal, nothing-wrong-with-them-people. Except the teaspoon rattled as she placed it on the saucer, giving away her ragged nerves. Jack brought the teapot and toast over and sat down. Jane would have preferred him to sit on the other chair so that she wouldn't have to see over his shoulder—but too late now. She sat opposite Jack and tried to absorb herself with his blue eyes. They looked tired but intense. She locked eyes with them, and Jack smiled warmly in response.

"Do you trust me Jane?" he asked.

Jane was taken aback. Even though Jack had secrets and didn't like to talk about feelings—she knew he loved her. "Of course. Yes."

"I'll always protect you Jane."

"I know that Jack, and I know I'm only little, but I'll protect you as well."

Jack smiled in response. "I've got a plan Jane that I'm working on. It's not quite finished so I don't want to tell you about it yet. I just need you to trust me though. Can you do that?"

Jane looked into Jack's blue eyes and then flicked her eyes over his shoulder at Death stood just behind him. Her Death. Her angel of death that Jack couldn't see. Her version of Death that had stood sentry at the foot of her bed last night, unmoving in the dark, and now following her around like a bodyguard.

Death didn't move so Jane looked back at Jack. The answer was obvious anyway: she didn't want to live in a world in which she didn't trust Jack. "Yes, I trust you." Jane replied.

"Thank you. It'll be okay," said Jack.

Jane nodded and poured a dash of milk into both cups. Her hands had stopped shaking. "It had better be," she said and smiled.

Jack picked up the teapot. "I can't imagine a world without you Jane. I'll make sure that you're okay. Tea?"

Jane nodded and they both checked the tea that poured from the spout into Jane's cup for the right depth of colour.

"Perfect." Jane smiled.

"If there's one thing I can cook, it's tea."

"Cook? Making tea isn't cooking!"

"What about toast then? Surely that counts as cooking?"

"Only in your head could tea and toast count as cooking Jack—" a normal conversation in a room with Death watching, mixed with a conversation about trust; our normal was a long way from most people's normal, Jane thought, "—so, when will you tell me your plan?" Jane decided a little probing wouldn't be a betrayal of the trust she had agreed to place in Jack.

Jack looked thoughtful before replying in a measured voice. "I just haven't quite got it all worked out yet. As soon as I do, you'll be the first to know."

"Promise?"

"Promise."

Jane took a sip of tea. "Hmm, delicious. Have you thought about writing a cookbook? Tea for one, tea for two, tea for three. Then tea and toast for one, for two, for three... you must have loads of material."

Jack spluttered as he was taking his own sip and spilt tea on the table. "Funny!" He stood to get a cloth.

Jane gasped and wanted to shout out a warning but just managed to stop herself. Jack turned and walked towards the sink to grab the orange dishcloth that hung from the tap. With Jack's back to her, Jane's hand rushed to cover her mouth as her eyes opened wide in fear. She wanted to shout out a warning. She desperately wanted to call Jack back. But

130

how could she, without giving away the presence of her angel of death?

"I'll get it," she called out, far too late.

"Ha!" Jack laughed, almost at the sink. He reached out and put his hand straight through the angel of death's battered breastplate. He reached through Death, retrieved the dishcloth then turned back and walked away, completely oblivious to Death's presence.

"Brr." Jack shivered on his way back. "There's a draught here somewhere. Don't worry I've got it." He held up his prize then wiped up the tea. "I'll keep that here just in case." He placed the cloth on the table and resumed drinking his tea.

Jane kept silent as the tension in her reduced and her heartrate slowed to somewhere near normal, while Jack alternated between his tea and toast. She looked at her hands; palm down, then palm up, palm down, palm up—as if they might reveal answers. Anything was better than looking up and seeing Death over Jack's shoulder.

"What do you want?" she asked Death.

"Eh?" Jack replied.

"Oh, sorry. I was just thinking out loud," she replied and shrugged. "Maybe we could just run away. Maybe Death wouldn't follow us." She leant forward, her voice cracking. "I can't take it Jack... I just can't." Her face crumpled like melted wax, and tears welled up from her green eyes. She hadn't wanted to breakdown in front of Jack, but Death's constant presence was whittling away at her resolve. She thought of the mirror in her room. The window to her soul, in which she allowed herself to look at her real self. The real Jane—that's where she could break—not here in front of Jack. She gulped it back down. Swallowed the fear and the anguish, bringing it back under control and burying it deep inside herself where Jack couldn't see it, hidden and silent. She would let it out later. Tonight, when she looked in her mirror again.

Jack reached across to hold her hands in his. "I've got a plan Jane. Just give me a little time. I can end this, I'm sure of it... just... just trust me."

"Okay... I'm sorry... Death's behind you Jack."

"What!" Jack jumped up and span around. "Where?"

"By the sink Jack. My Death. My angel of death. She's following me everywhere now... it's like she's guarding me."

"Guarding you?"

"Yeah, like a bodyguard. She just hangs around watching. She appeared last night just after the cows in the field got spooked."

"I can't see her."

"I know Jack. I know you can't. She's driving me crazy Jack. I don't know what she wants with me? I don't know why she isn't killing me? What's going on Jack? Why are you, Dave and Ginny getting killed and I'm getting protected? She's not even telling me about the balance being wrong anymore, she just follows me around."

Jack looked horrified. "I don't know Jane," he gulped. "I've got to go."

"What?"

"Sorry."

"Jack!"

"I'll see you later alright. I'll email."

"Jack..." but he was gone. He hadn't even finished his tea.

Chapter 22

The pig trough in the empty pigsty behind the stables was out of sight of the farmhouse. The sty was caked in hard mud, baked dry by the spring sun into uneven canyons and potholes. The pigs that wallowed here through autumn and winter were out in their fields.

Alfred looked around, surmising that he must have been carried here, or more likely dragged while unconscious, by Fat Joe.

The rustling mass in front of Alfred drew his attention. It moved in a way that resisted his eyes' focus as the spiders clambered over each other, trying to reach the raw meat inside. The mass heaved and rolled like waves in a broiling, black sea. And like sand, Fat Joe's body was taken away piece by piece until the sea withdrew and revealed the shining, white skeleton underneath. The clothes were untouched, and bones stuck out from trouser legs and shirt cuffs like straw from a scarecrow. Fat Joe's skull stared unblinking at the sky, slack-jawed and emptied of all the hatred and cruelty that it had once contained. Alfred paid it no more attention than he would roadkill in the gutter.

The spiders parted to allow him passage across the sty. He walked through them and peered around the corner of the stables to see the farmhouse, but there was no sign of Mildred. The farmhouse door was closed, and the windows were as vacant of life as Fat Joe's picked clean eye sockets.

Alfred stared out while thinking about what he should do. He was at a crossroads. He could turn left and take this farm for his own; he could turn right and disappear into the countryside to forge a new life; or he could continue straight on, along the path that started with Fat Joe's death and ended with the destruction of Middle Gratestone and everyone that lived there.

His newly restored connection to the spiders and other creatures gave him the power to decide his own destiny. He was no longer just a thirteen-year-old boy. He was a commander of an army—a spider army! He could march at its head and take whatever he wanted from whoever he wanted. Power gave him opportunity. Power gave him freewill. Power gave him choice.

Alfred's mind buzzed with ideas as the spiders scuttled around waiting for direction. But really, Alfred had no choice.

One idea, one option, rose above all the others. It smothered optimism and stifled opportunity. It crushed hope and reduced Alfred's future to a landscape as barren as his past. There would be no joy for Alfred, no happiness, no love to blossom and fill his life with colour. Revenge was his only choice. Its fire burned within him. It had been lit over one-hundred-years ago and only the complete destruction of all that he hated would extinguish the furnace from which its dark flames spewed.

"Revenge!" Alfred spat, and set upon the path that led straight ahead.

He crossed the open ground to the farmhouse, eyeing the windows as he went. He walked in plain sight, confident that his role had changed from prey to hunter. He no longer needed to walk in the shadows and look over his shoulder for danger because he had power now that put him right at the top of the food-chain. Power that he would use, cruelly and viciously without mercy, to turn his enemies into skeleton mannequins—clothed, but devoid of flesh, modelling a death pose in their last choice of outfit... just like Fat Joe was doing in the pigsty.

There was no sign of Mildred, so Alfred paused at the farmhouse door, then with a smirk, hit on a plan. He quietly cracked open the door and listened, then using his mind, called forward one of the rats that lived in the stables. It scurried over, bound up the doorstep, paused momentarily sniffing the air at the doorway then snuck inside.

Alfred remained poised at the door, focusing in his mind on what the rat could see, hear and smell with its sharp senses. The hall and kitchen were clear, but the rat picked up a noise from upstairs—regular—repeating every few seconds, deep and rumbling. The rat rushed silently up the stairs, crossed the landing and paused at the bedroom door. Mildred was snoring in bed, recovering from being woken early, and oblivious to Alfred and the death of her husband. The rat stood sentry at the door while Alfred moved into the kitchen to gather supplies. He pulled a small backpack from a hook on the door and quickly filled it with a fresh loaf of bread, a hunk of ham, some apples, cheese and a large bottle of water. Then he crossed into the lounge, grabbed a blanket used as a throw on the sofa and stuffed it into the pack, and finally rammed a coat in on top and fastened the straps tight.

A set of knives hung from a magnetic strip on the kitchen wall. Alfred slid one into a side pocket on the backpack and headed for the back door. The key was in the lock, so he locked the door and pocketed the key. He took one quick glance around and headed for the front door, taking the key from the inside lock and putting it in the outside lock as he quietly stepped outside. His trap was almost ready to be sprung.

He ushered in another ten rats. They were sleek and fast, and their feet scratched at the doorstep as they leapt in, then they were gone, scurrying around in the interior. Alfred closed and locked the front door.

Smiling to himself, he walked around the side of the house and retrieved the hammer and nails from the shed. The house was a standard shape and size. Downstairs there was one front door and one back, and eight windows, two on each side of the house. Upstairs there were another eight windows, two on each side.

Alfred went to the nearest window, took out a nail and held the point on the wooden bottom edge of the window. Tap, tap, bang, bang and the nail secured the bottom edge of the window to the windowsill. Alfred ran to the next window. Tap, tap, bang, bang. Then the next.

A warning appeared in his mind. A vision of Mildred lifting herself up in bed—woken by something she had not yet identified. Tap, tap, bang, bang. Mildred heard the banging and swung her legs off the bed. Tap, tap, bang, bang. She walked to the bedroom window and looked out. Tap, tap, bang, bang. She craned left and right but Alfred was around the other side of the house. Tap, tap, bang, bang. Mildred turned to leave the bedroom to find out what had interrupted her sleep, determined to give someone a piece of her mind. She paused to check herself in the mirror. Tap, tap, bang, bang.

"That is quite enough of that noise," she said to her reflection. Tap, tap, bang, bang. Alfred was finished with the windows. The rat that had been watching Mildred, pulled back into the shadows to allow Mildred to leave the room.

Alfred stood at the front door and banged a nail into the doorjamb for good measure and then ran around the back of the house.

Mildred trudged down the stairs—still slow and woozy from being recently woken. Tap, tap, bang, bang from the backdoor. Mildred looked at the door, walked towards it and tried the handle. Locked. She went to turn the key, but it wasn't there. Puzzlement creased her brow and sleep fell away from her in sudden warning. A scuttling sound twitched her head around, but nothing was there, so she walked quickly to the front door and tried the handle. Locked—the key missing.

She banged the door hard with the palm of her hand.

"Joe?" she half shouted then paused to listen. "Joe?" Mildred banged the door again then pushed at it in frustration. Deciding to look out of a window, she headed for the kitchen. The rats that had been hiding in shoes, under furniture and behind plant pots scurried after her, their scratching claws silent under the cover of Mildred's heavier tread. They scattered as they entered the kitchen, again folding themselves into the small dark places that afforded them cover.

Mildred looked out the window. She could see no movement in the courtyard and surrounding stables, even the trees in the distance were motionless in the light breeze, only the gentle fluttering of leaves gave them away. She tried to peer to the sides but couldn't see down the outside wall of the house, so she heaved at the window to open it, but it didn't budge. She heaved again and succeeded in pulling her lower back which she had to stretch off with a hand on her hip.

"Where are you Joe?" she grumbled, placing the palm of her other hand on the glass as if gently touching his face. She felt a tear coming. A sense of doom welled up—something terrible had happened—she knew it as surely as she knew the sun would set tonight and rise again tomorrow. Her vision swam as her eyes filled then she jumped at a blur of movement and bang on the glass as another hand met hers, palm-to-palm, from the other side of the pane.

Alfred appeared. His eyes were darker than Mildred remembered, hooded in the shadow of the farmhouse. Malice poured from them as if the dam that had held it back had burst. Alfred openly sneered, all pretence of compliance was gone. Mildred withdrew her hand and stared back, unable to tear her gaze from the undisguised hatred.

Alfred bent down and retrieved a paintbrush and paint tin from the ground. He held them up for Mildred to see, then dipped the brush in the tin and wrote in big red letters on the window, 'Death'. He wrote carefully, forming the letters backwards from right to left so that Mildred could read them from her side of the glass. She watched in horror as the red paint dripped down the window like blood.

Alfred wrote another word under the first, 'by'.

He smiled now and raised his eyebrows as if encouraging Mildred to guess the last word. She shook her head, not wanting to know what it was. Alfred shrugged and dipped the paintbrush once more then wrote at the bottom of the window in letters twice the size as the others, 'Rat'. He stepped back to admire his handiwork.

The words he had written in blood red adorned the window, obscuring his view of Mildred within the farmhouse, but it didn't matter because he could still see her through the black eyes of the many rats that watched from the shadows. Alfred started to fill their minds with suggestion.

'*You are hungry. You need to feed. The woman tastes good. She will fill your empty stomachs. She is dangerous. She will kill your babies. You must stop her—you must kill her... kill her now before she kills your babies... before she kills you. Kill her now. Feed!*'

Alfred fed their minds with his thoughts, filling them with every reason he could think of for them to attack, until they broke and surged forward in a rush of scratching claws and sharp biting teeth. Alfred walked away and left them to their frenzy. He had a long walk ahead and the sun was already getting high in the sky.

Chapter 23

The first rat that reached Mildred sunk its teeth into the big toe on Mildred's left foot. The toe protruded from Mildred's sandals. It was red and round and looked far too juicy for the rat to consider seeking a vein or artery that might result in a quicker kill. The toe had wriggled in the sandal like a pink slug while Mildred had watched Alfred paint on the window. The rat had almost attacked before Alfred had filled its mind with suggestion, such was the temptation.

As it bit down, its sharp ears could hear the other rats rushing into the fray, followed by Mildred's piercing scream of pain. But it was the first, so it claimed the big toe for its own. Blood squirted into its mouth in a delicious gush. The rat released its grip to bite again but Mildred yanked her foot back and stamped down hard, breaking the rat's neck and crushing its skull. It lay there, motionless, as its heart pointlessly tried to carry on beating, unaware of the catastrophic injury to the head and neck.

The next two rats to reach Mildred leapt onto her legs and used their sharp claws to race up the back of her trousers. Mildred turned, flailing her arms and saw a rat leap from the kitchen worktop. She caught it in mid-air and instantly regretted it as the rat sunk its teeth into her finger. Other rats reached her feet and rushed up her trousers while the first two reached her hair and tried to bite into her scalp and the back of her neck; one found an earlobe and bit right through.

Mildred slammed the rat in her hand down hard on the worktop, crushing its ribs but the rat hung on to Mildred's finger, so she brought her hand down hard again, then twice more until it released its grip.

Rats were all over her now. They had found gaps in her clothing and were biting at her stomach, trying to rip away her flesh and bury into her abdomen; they ripped and tore and forced their heads inside her.

Mildred screamed and grabbed a rat from her face that was dangerously close to her eyes, then grabbed another that was savaging her ear. With both hands full and rats biting her all over her body, she did the only thing she could do. She forced the head end of the rat in her right hand into her mouth and bit down hard. The rat's neck broke first then blood spurted into her mouth as she gripped with her teeth and ripped the rat's body away, leaving the severed head in her mouth. She dropped the rat's body and spat out the head.

The rat in her left hand was biting into the web of her thumb, but the pain from the rats burrowing into her abdomen blotted it out, so Mildred ignored it and grabbed the two rats eating at her stomach and crushed them both by gripping their bodies with such ferocity that their insides exploded from either end. Mildred dropped them, then grabbed the rat that was chewing at the web of her left hand with her other hand so that she held each end of the rat then she ripped it apart like a Christmas cracker. Blood spurted from both ends as she dropped the two halves on the floor.

She grabbed the remaining rats still eating at her body and ripped them apart one-by-one, screaming in pain and fury as she destroyed them all.

Then it stopped. Mildred was alone, panting in the kitchen as blood dripped from her many wounds. She remained where she was, looking around at the rat carcasses that littered the floor—waiting for any remaining rats to attack, but the house was silent.

Mildred put her head back and howled in anguish and pain. Sobs overwhelmed her, and the pain of the bites almost made her knees give way. But she was stronger than that. She would not fall.

She staggered across the kitchen and pulled her first aid kit from a cupboard. It was well stocked and all the contents in-date: she always saw to that. She started to apply dressings and bandages to stem the blood flow that seemed to be coming from everywhere, moaning in pain as she touched her own ragged flesh.

A dark anger descended over her as she worked. This was not acceptable. Her kitchen was a mess—her hair was a mess—her clothes were ruined. Alfred was going to pay for what he had done to her. She was going to find him, and she was going to kill him.

Mildred picked up the heavy, steel mop-bucket that she used to keep her floors immaculate. She looked at the crimson blood and the rat carcasses for a moment as if contemplating cleaning up, then threw the steel bucket as hard as she could at the kitchen window. She would clean later.

The glass shattered, destroying Alfred's artwork. Then Mildred grabbed the mop and used it to put out the glass from the remaining panels until all trace of Alfred's words were gone. She looked through to the outside world. Atop a hill, about a mile away, she could see the distant figure of Alfred walking away from the farm.

She gauged the direction in which he was heading. "I know where you're going," she said.

She finished cleaning herself and patching her wounds then went into the hall and opened the door to the under-stair cupboard. She reached inside, up behind the door, to pull out a long leather bag that had been lying on two hooks. She also retrieved a cardboard box from a shelf and took both to the kitchen table.

She sat down and reverently unzipped the bag. The smell of leather and gun oil mixed in a very comforting way as she pulled the zip the full length of the bag to reveal Fat Joe's double-barrelled shotgun. She broke the shotgun open and loaded it with two shells from the cardboard box then snapped it shut.

"It's time to go hunting. But first, where's Joe?"

Chapter 24

Jane washed the cups, saucers, plates and cutlery that she and Jack had used. It was cathartic. She used the task like a toddler used a comforter, and slowly she calmed while trying her best to avoid catching sight of Death stood motionless in her kitchen.

The constant presence of Death allowed Jane to normalise the experience and gain a little perspective on what Death was doing here. Slowly, strands of individual thoughts strung together into something coherent. Jane's mind speeded up as her dread drifted away, enabling her to put her brain to use.

What was Death? She wondered. Jane couldn't sense good or evil. Death was simply present. And despite the manifestation of Death as a battle-hardened angel replete in scarred armour, Jane did not feel directly threatened. Death was a soldier, a tool; here to serve a purpose without self-gratification or malice. Death was a function. There was no evil, just purpose.

Someone, somewhere, a long time ago had set Death on this path and she remained on it now, steadfast and absolute in her purpose. Unfaltering. Unwavering. But why appear to us now? Jane thought. What's gone wrong?

"You saved Alfred, didn't you?" Jane looked at Death. "And that set something in motion. You saved Alfred and you shouldn't have... and maybe you could have got away with it, but you made another mistake. You brought Ginny back and then Alfred back, but you were so focused on saving Alfred that you didn't realise the numbers were wrong."

Jane continued to look at Death, but Death showed no reaction. "There's a consequence!" Jane realised. "If it stays unbalanced then there is a consequence. But what is it? And who holds you to account? Who do you have to explain your actions to?"

Jane kept going with her logic. "It must be a higher power. So, God? The Devil? Both? Or, someone else? Both," she decided, answering her own question. "So, if you are supposed to take the soul away from here when people die, to wherever... what happens when you don't?"

She sat down, lost in her thought process. She didn't know if she was right or wrong, but her thoughts were leading somewhere. "Maybe there was an agreement—a deal of some sort. Maybe between God and the Devil. Maybe they leave us alone here on Earth if you deliver souls to them. Maybe you broke the deal. Oh my God what happens then? Can the Devil come here? Is the barrier between life and death gone? Between good and evil? Can Hell come to Earth? Oh my God... WHAT HAVE YOU DONE?" Jane screamed.

She pushed her chair back and rounded on Death, pointing her finger straight at Death's scarred armour breastplate.

"What have you done?" she repeated, prodding Death so hard her finger bent on the rigid metal. "This is your mess. Fix it. Without us!"

The angel of death shook her head.

"Take Alfred then, he shouldn't be alive. He's the mistake. Take him back."

The angel of death shook her head then slowly raised a claw to point at Jane.

"Me? No, that's not fair. Ginny... take Ginny."

Death continued to point at Jane.

"I'm not dead. You can't take me."

Death didn't waver, but the pointed claw seemed to convey insistence—certainty.

"I won't kill myself, if that's what you want... and you can't make me."

Death shook her head.

"Wait, you really can't kill me? No of course you can't... and you can't make me kill myself either. Wait. You want the others to kill me! Then you can take me away and the balance is restored. They won't do it. Jack won't do it, I know he won't."

The angel of death nodded. A voice appeared in Jane's head. It was her own voice, her inner voice, and it spoke to her. "All will be restored to balance."

"No! I don't believe it. They won't kill me... and you can't kill me... and they won't... Jack will look after me. I'm sure he will." Jane reached for the chair. It was behind her, so she waved her hand around, blindly searching for it as she stepped backwards keeping her eyes on Death. "I'm sure he will." She found the chair and sat down heavily. "Yes, he will. He'll look after me. He won't hurt me."

She was breathing fast but lightly in shallow breaths. The feeling was familiar to her—it was panic. Her pulse raced, and light-headedness washed over her. Suddenly she felt sick and rushed for the edge of the sink. She grabbed it and threw up violently. Stars flashed in her eyes and her stomach heaved until it was empty. Once it had stopped she rested her forehead on her white knuckles that still gripped the side of the sink. The stars diminished, and her stomach calmed. She stayed there like a statue until her pulse and breathing returned to normal. The chaotic thoughts that rushed around her mind also slowed and calmed until only one remained... Jack is going to kill me.

"Jack is going to kill me," she said it out loud.

Death nodded in confirmation.

"Well if he does kill me then it will be a kindness because I don't want to live if Jack wants to kill me. So, either he'll do it, and that's fine, or he won't, and that's fine as well." Jane's words tumbled out. "It would be nice to know which though, so I guess I need to get on and find out. Next question then. How do I find out?" Jane asked it out loud, but she wasn't looking at Death for the answers anymore, she was asking herself.

Chapter 25

Alfred knew the way to Middle Gratestone from Fat Joe's farm. In the farmhouse, Fat Joe kept a map in a picture frame on the wall. Alfred had studied it many times and committed the route home to memory. It was a long way by road, but as the crow flies, straight across a corner of Dartmoor, it was only five miles.

He had walked on the moor a few times with his father and knew the ground over which he had to travel was tough. There were bogs in the low areas, craggy tors with seemingly endless uphill climbs to reach them, sharp gorse that snatched at skin and clothes, and tufted grass on which it was too easy to turn an ankle.

But Alfred felt good—he felt confident. Now was his time. Now was the moment when things started to go right for him. Now was his moment of glory. His moment to take back what belonged to him. His moment to shine. *And how he would shine!* Like an explosion, or the centre of a ball of fire. Alfred would shine in his moment and destroy everything he hated. He would flatten Middle Gratestone and the thieves and murderers that lived there, then he would build a new life for himself on top of the smoking rubble. He would rise like a phoenix from the ashes of his enemies and fly high in the sky over them all. Now was his time.

Something barred his way, stopping him from walking any further and interrupting his reverie, so he looked up.

150

His thoughts of conquest had been so absorbing that he had failed to see the perimeter fence until it halted his progress. He took the unplanned stop as an opportunity to look at the sun and gauge his direction of travel from its position in the sky. He could see a ruin on a hill about a mile distant—it was in the right direction, so he set a path straight towards it and set off once again.

Easy as cake, he thought as he climbed the fence and headed for the ruin. A carpet of spiders followed behind him like a bridal trail flowing across the ground. Up close the skulls on the backs of the spiders were clearly visible, but from a distance the spiders merged together into an amorphous black mass that flowed hypnotically like black oil over the contours of the land. Overhead a hawk screeched while crows kept a respectful distance, and behind Alfred's black trail, ran sleek rats that flitted in and out of view in the tufted grass.

Alfred felt like whistling. He felt a stirring of happiness, an undercurrent that swelled as he walked away from the farm. It would be easy to fall for its seductive charm, but Alfred had business to attend to—nasty business. So, he ruthlessly quashed it and thought about revenge, brutality, blood and gore. Those were the thoughts that he needed to sustain his resolve through the tasks at hand. He must remain strong and hateful. Later, when he had killed them all, then he could rest and be happy. Then he could try and live a normal life. The type of life that most people had but took for granted. A boring life, uneventful and safe.

Alfred's feet squelched as the grass sank underneath him. The grass was woven like a raft over a boggy area at the foot of the hill. There were many areas like these on Dartmoor. Alfred knew if he broke through the grass raft that he would sink into the mud below and be lost forever. So, he skirted around it to a line of rocks then, once on solid ground, headed once more to the ruin on the hill.

He spotted a worn path that weaved around the rocky outcrops on the hillside. It was likely made by sheep and the Dartmoor ponies that roamed here. Alfred followed the path and let the steep incline warm his muscles. He put his head down and concentrated on his footing. As he pushed upwards in the heat of the sun, his feet passed over brown dusty earth, dried out lichen patched on rocks and tough straw-like grass. The breeze was less here in the lee of the hill causing Alfred to sweat. He had lost sight of the ruin due to the clutter of crags, so he doggedly followed the path and watched his feet eat up the climb. The path meandered around, taking the easiest route up the hill.

Alfred stopped atop a rock to take a drink. Looking back, he could see the farm in the centre of the flat-bottomed valley, but he wasn't sure of his direction at all. Sighing, he turned and continued upwards until the hill levelled and crested out. He looked around and saw the ruin. He'd missed it in the maze of rocks, but it was only about two-hundred-yards to his right, so he walked over to it then checked the sun to get his direction.

The sun was at its zenith, so it must be midday and therefore Alfred couldn't discern any sense of direction from its position. So, he put the farm to his back and sited his direction along the ruin into the distance. He could see a high rocky tor; the top was about a mile away. It would be a tough climb going straight to it, but if he contoured around he might get lost. Even with a spider army at his disposal he didn't want to spend a night on the moors. Exhaustion and exposure were real risks even in June. Alfred took another sip of water then headed for the high tor.

"Come on guys," he called out to the creatures following him. "The sooner we get there, the sooner you can eat."

As Alfred passed over the crest of the hill he started to descend, affording him a view of the deep valley that lay between him and the tor in front. The green flank of the hill was probably only a quarter of a mile away; if he could walk across on a bridge over the valley it would only take him five minutes. But the way he had to go, deep down into the valley, it would probably be an hour before he got back to the same height on the opposite hill. He realised he wouldn't be able to see the tor from the bottom of the valley, so he picked out a rocky outcrop in line with the tor and headed for that.

The descent was steep causing a punishing constant, jarring of his thighs every time he stepped down. Alfred was fit though from the hard work on Fat Joe's farm, so he stuck to the task with a doggedness that had seen him through the many trials he had previously suffered.

"It's better than being hit by Fat Joe," he said to his entourage.

Thirty minutes later he was at the small stream that splashed through the sharp valley. He found a crossing point between two rocks that he could use and once over he cut back to the stream and sank down next to the clear water. He thought it was probably drinkable, but in case it wasn't, he just splashed it on his head and the back of his neck until the burn from the sun faded.

Alfred drank from his bottle then headed for the outcrop he had picked out earlier. This is going to be a hard climb, he thought, as he started up on another animal track that wound up the hill like a snake.

"I bet Fat Joe never did this climb," he chortled. "Nor Mildred." At the thought of her, she sprang to the front of his mind. She was strong and fit and he wondered how she was getting on with the rats. He had lost his connection with them as he had walked away from the farm. He had worked them up into a frenzy before he had left but the winner of the battle between Mildred and ten rats was not certain.

"Maybe I should have sent more in?" he thought and looked to the rats following him. "No, I'll need you guys. If Mildred is still... alive... we'll deal with her... later." Alfred panted out the words as he fought the hill. His thighs were burning, and he still hadn't made it to the outcrop. He could see it, but there was still a lot of hill to climb.

He thought of the baker that had refused him a loaf of bread, and of the baker's descendant, Jane. "I... hate... you," he said, putting his hatred of Jane into the effort of climbing.

He thought of the policeman that had made him homeless, and the policeman's descendant, Jack. "I... hate... you."

He thought of the mayor that had schemed and plotted to ruin his family, and the mayor's descendant, Ginny. "I... hate you."

He thought of the vicar that had denied him shelter in the church, and the vicar's descendant, Dave. "I... hate... you."

His hatred ate up the distance to the outcrop and soon he was there, catching his breath and drinking cold water from his bottle. He looked back to the ruin and the farm further on, set his course on a line from them, then headed up the steep climb to the tor.

"I... hate... you... I... hate... you... I... hate... you." He breathed hard and his lungs burned but his rage gave strength to his legs and he continued his ascent. As he climbed the wind picked up and blew over the sweat on his clothes and matted hair. It was cooling at first but the higher he got the colder it became. His body was still warmed by the climb, but the wind blustered around pushing him off balance and making his hands and ears cold.

He pushed on until he reached the ragged rocks of the tor. They protruded from the green top of the hill like a crooked grey tooth crumbling in decay. Alfred picked his way around the rocks to look out over Dartmoor. To his left, the hills stretched out for miles. High tors were dotted around like gravestones atop the hills, and deep scars of valleys crossed between them ensuring the journey from tor-to-tor deterred all but the hardiest of adventurers. Gorse bushes, flowering in patches of yellow, carpeted the sides of the lower slopes, and rocks were peppered here and there. Together they hindered progress in anything resembling a straight line. It was tough country.

Not that way, thought Alfred, remembering the map in the hall. He looked half-right. A valley stretched away from him, its gentle slopes green and inviting. At the far end of the valley, at the very edge of the moor, there was a town. Alfred recognised it, even though it was one-hundred-years since he had last looked down on it from the moors.

"Found you!" Middle Gratestone was laid out waiting for him, plump and fat, like a Christmas turkey ready to be devoured. Alfred pulled into the lee of a rock to escape the cold wind and opened his backpack. He pulled out the hunk of ham and loaf of bread he had taken from the farmhouse, and tucked into them, alternately taking big bites from each as he surveyed the town and plotted his revenge.

Chapter 26

They met in secret. Each one of them went a different route to get there. Each one careful to avoid anywhere that Jane might have been—not that she left the house much these days. They arrived within minutes of each other and settled quickly on the wooden chairs around the table. It was a long two minutes before anybody spoke.

"What are we doing?"

"That's obvious isn't it."

"I just think that someone should say it so there is no doubt about what we are discussing here."

"Go ahead."

"I know we are all thinking it. I know we arranged this meeting to discuss it, but someone needs to say it for it to be real. I don't want to be that person."

"If you don't want to say it, how could you possibly do it?"

There was a pause while the question was considered.

"I don't know if I could do it... that's the truth"

"Let's start with an easier question than if we should do it, or who should do it," a third voice cut in.

"Okay like what?"

"Like, where should we do it?"

"Easy. The graveyard."

"Yep, the graveyard."

"Okay then, how should we do it?"

"How?"

"Yes, how?"

The clock on the wall ticked the seconds away. It sounded loud in the silence.

"We hit her with a rock, that might make it look like an accident."

"How hard would you hit her?"

"What? Very hard of course."

"Well how can you be sure of killing her with one hit? It's got to be one hit for it to look like an accident."

"I don't know..."

"Exactly. We have to do it in a way that we can be sure will work... and that we won't get caught."

"Suffocation."

"Poison."

"Drowning."

"Not drowning. Too hard to do in a graveyard."

"Suffocation or poison then."

"Suffocation."

"Suffocation."

"What with? A plastic bag over her mouth? A hand... your hand... my hand? Strangle her? Come on, who's going to be able to do that?

"Yeah, I couldn't.

"Poison then"

"What poison would we use?"

"Some mushrooms are poisonous."

"Yes, but which ones? They all look the same we might accidently give her ones that weren't poisonous."

"She doesn't like mushrooms anyway, she won't eat them."

"What about deadly nightshade?"

"I don't think we can feed her anything. It's not a picnic we're going on, and if we manage to get her to eat something poisonous it might take too long to take effect. She could run away and die somewhere else... or not die at all."

"Yeah, and if she doesn't eat it what then, are we just going to stand around like lemons."

"I know a poison."

"What poison?"

"My dad keeps one at home, and it's got an antidote."

"We don't want to save her, we just want to kill her!"

"I know but you said yourself how do we get her to eat anything? Well the way to get her to do something is for us all to do it. So, we all take the poison."

"What?!" the other two stared in disbelief.

"Okay, let me spell it out. Us three meet first... and take the antidote. Then we meet Jane and we all take a drink of the poison. We could do it as a toast. 'Here's to the end of Death,' something like that. I could mix the poison in with something strong, like brandy or whisky, to disguise the taste, then we take a drink... all of us. But we've already had the antidote so we're okay. Jane hasn't so she dies."

There was silence for a little while as the other two thought about what had been proposed.

"Okay how do we know that the antidote will work?"

"It's all about dosage, I just need to get the dosage right, that's all. Then it will definitely work."

"Okay, and why do you have poison?"

"Like I said, my dad has it, but he told me never to keep poison at home unless you also keep the antidote... that's why he has both. And he uses it for rat traps, but there's loads of it... definitely enough to kill a person."

"And just to be sure here, how can you be certain you can get the antidote dosage right, and then the poison dosage right so that only Jane dies?"

"You two aren't doing chemistry at school, are you?"

"No."

"No."

"Exactly. But I am. This is the way to do it, and it will definitely work. We take the antidote. We give her the poison. We talk and stuff until she dies then we go home and leave her. If we do it late tonight no one will even know that we were there."

They paused again while the enormity of what they had just talked about sunk in.

"Alright, another easy question before we try and answer if and who. Why should we do it?"

"To stop the damn dreams of course."

"Yes, to stop the dreams. And to stop Death killing us in our dreams, and now killing us when we're awake. And to stop him telling us that nature needs to be rebalanced. I can't take it anymore. So, we kill Jane...she's given up on life anyway. Then we hope, and this is a big hope, that Death comes and takes Jane and that's it, nature is rebalanced, or whatever it is that the damn dreams mean."

"Well that answers the why. As for the if? I say yes. We should do it."

"Yes, we should do it"

"Okay, yes."

"Only one question left then. Who is going to kill Jane?"

"I'll do it. I'll give her the poison. It's mine anyway and I'm doing the dosage, but you both must agree to do exactly what I say. And I don't want Jane to suffer so don't tell her we've given her poison even when she's dying. I don't want her to know we killed her."

"Okay, agreed."

"Yep. Agreed."

"I'll get her to the graveyard for eight o'clock... what time shall we meet."

"Ten minutes before, that'll be enough. Right I'm off to sort the doses out. See you soon."

"See ya."

"Yep."

Chapter 27

After eating lunch in the lee of a rock, Alfred put away the remains of the ham and bread then looked around the countryside. The spiders were huddled nearby, clumped together in a seething ball underneath an overhang of the great jutting tor. Their movement was mesmerising. They crawled over each other, individuals disappearing and reappearing as the ball ebbed and flowed. Alfred stared into the mass and felt his mind drift into a daydream.

He imagined forcing Jane to thrust an arm into the ball and hold it there while the spiders stripped her flesh. He heard her screams in his mind. Then another version of Jane's screams joined the first and screamed as well, then another and another until a whole choir of Janes screamed in his mind. The sound became overpowering, cutting through him and setting his teeth on edge. It was too much. He forced Jane's head into the ball and the screams cut off in an instant as if a conductor had silenced the choir with the wave of a wand.

He smirked at the scale of his inventiveness then pulled his gaze from the spiders and continued roving his eyes across the vista before him. The rats rustled around in the tufted grass—mostly out of sight. The crows were dotted around on crags like blotches of black ink on tissue, their feathers blustering in the wind that gusted across the moor while the hawk glided lazily far above, riding the gusts and thermals to stay aloft without any effort.

They're not enough, thought Alfred. I need a bigger army. I need more of them all, and I need some giant ones to lead the way. Giant spiders like I had before. Yes, that's what I need—perhaps I should have turned Fat Joe into a giant fat spider, I could have ridden him into battle... ha-ha. No, he deserved death. I need someone else—someone new. I need to find people and turn them into giant creatures to help me wage war on Middle Gratestone. Yes, think big Alfred... think giant!

A speckle of colour like discarded confetti caught his eye in the valley. Red, green, blue and orange shapes were dotted around in a field just on the outskirts of Middle Gratestone. Alfred squinted and was just able to make out a group of tents with people scurrying about between them.

Perfect, he thought. I can turn them into spiders like before, then lead a great spider army into Middle Gratestone to destroy everything. Alfred smiled then stood and hoisted up his pack. It wouldn't take long to reach the campsite. He could see a woodland alongside it that he could use to disguise his approach. Then he could send the spiders into the field, one tent at a time, until they turned everyone there into something he could use.

Alfred chose a dirt path that wound down the hill into the valley. His legs had stiffened while he had eaten lunch, so they hurt until warmed by the descent. It was easier going this side of the tor, the slope was gentler. Soon tufted grass

163

and spiky gorse, gave way to stunted trees grown bent over to one side, blown that way by the prevailing wind. They looked like hunched men all facing the same way, sheltering their faces from the wind's incessant bite. In their turn, the hunched men gave way to tall strong oak trees that rose from moss beds and hid Alfred's approach. He kept in the woods, away from the fields that lined the centre of the valley and skulked in the cool, sultry cover of the oaks.

He started to hear cries on the wind. They were joyful—the sound of children playing—soon though they would be cries of terror. Alfred felt no guilt for his prey—no sympathy—he closed that part of his mind off, barricaded it in with his anger and thirst for revenge. One day when he had the luxury of comfort and happiness he would allow the guilt to wash over him. But not today. Today he would wash away the injustice of his past with the blood of the town that had betrayed him.

He was close now. He could see glimpses of colour through the tree trunks. Children's voices sang in the breeze, interspersed with deeper adult voices. Alfred would need to be careful. If this was to be his plan—to turn these people into creatures—and use them to invade Middle Gratestone, then he mustn't fail here at the first challenge.

Stealth is the key, he thought. I need to get into position then attack from everywhere all at once. Alfred looked down at the field through the eyes of the hawk and started to finalise his plan.

* * * *

Little Molly Wilson sat in an orange tent pitched against the side of the woodland underneath overhanging trees. Her dad had told her this would keep the tent cool—he was clever like that. He was outside now, playing football with her brother and cousins.

"Goal!" Someone shouted.

"Offside!" someone else. All the boys laughed, and a friendly argument began.

Molly's mum was in a deckchair out front enjoying the sun. She was quiet and still so Molly guessed she had her eyes shut. Molly was in the tent because the bright sun had been reflecting off the white pages of her book, so she had taken it inside and was now sat on her pink blanket. She was cross-legged with her book laid in front, her chin resting on her hands while her eyes ran along the lines of words. She followed the story of the boy brought up by animals in the jungle. She was so absorbed she didn't notice the spiders coming in through air gaps in the tent and climbing up the inside walls, positioning themselves ready to attack.

Across the field other tents slowly filled with spiders while rats circled the edge of the field and set up a perimeter guard to catch any runners. Silent crows kept watch from branches as the unseen army of spiders patiently positioned themselves.

Once the creatures were set, Alfred signalled the start of the attack—not to devour and rip apart though, but to poison and infect. The creatures needed to bite the people in the campsite and infect them with Alfred's evil intent so that they would bloat and transform into giant versions of the creatures that had bitten them then submit to Alfred's will. This was how Alfred would create his army. He had done it before and was certain that it would work.

Molly heard the sudden cacophony of crows cawing in the woodland. It was a terrible sound, like when Molly ran her fingernails down her chalkboard at home to annoy her brother. It was the sound of the end of days. A cry of such sorrow and pain that Molly stopped reading in an instant, and the football outside rolled to a stop, ignored by the boys that moments earlier had been giving chase.

The crows cawed of the darkness of a woodland at night, of the loss of hatchlings to a rook and of shadows that moved in an unwatched graveyard. They cawed of the things they knew that people didn't. They cawed, and Molly gasped at the horribleness of it, then screamed as the first spider landed on the open page of her book, followed by many more that landed in her hair and on her clothes.

Molly's mum rushed in. More spiders, waiting above the doorway dropped into her hair. Molly's dad came through as well and more dropped onto him. The spiders found soft flesh in which to inject their poison then dropped to the ground and scurried off. Molly's mum swatted them off her daughter, ignoring her own bites that burnt like fire. She squashed some and they fell away curling into balls, their legs broken and useless. But others found their mark and fulfilled their role. The attack was repeated across the field, and in less than one minute it was over. The crows silenced, and the surviving spiders hid away.

Molly staggered to her feet and stepped over her parents writhing on the ground. She wanted to see the sun. She forced her feet forward and moved into the warm light. A tall, dirty boy stood in front of her. His hair was matted and sticking up. Rivers of dried sweat tracked down the dirt on his face, creating clean lines of skin. His mouth twisted into a sneer as he looked at her. Molly's knees gave way as the poison coursed through her and she fell forward onto the grass, bucking and writhing as the transformation took hold. The last sound she heard was that of mocking laughter.

Chapter 28

Jane shut down her computer and waited while the screen turned to darkness. She wondered if dying would be like that. You were alive then a switch was clicked, and you were dead. Did everything just turn to darkness in an instant.

No, probably not, she thought. There will probably be pain, terror and lots of screaming. Lots and lots of screaming if it's my death. No way I'm going quietly. That's it though! She realised. 'Going' was the important word. We go somewhere when we die. People always talk about passing away, moving on or going to a better place. People don't talk about stopping, disappearing or switching off. No, Jane thought. They don't talk about death like an end, they talk about it like a journey. And they're right. Because I know there is an angel of death and she takes us somewhere else. So maybe dying isn't such a bad thing.

Jane looked over her shoulder. Death was stood at the foot of her bed. "So where do you take us when we die?" Jane asked, but Death remained impassive. The silent countenance annoyed Jane. "You're just a taxi. You don't scare me."

Death didn't respond, but somehow seemed more threatening without moving, so Jane decided to stop antagonising her. "They call you the Grim Reaper as well don't they... suits you. Very grim." She turned back to the blank computer that she had turned off once she had read the email from Jack. She thought about what he had said.

'*Meeting at 8PM at the church. We need to talk again. Dave and Ginny will be there. Come alone. Jack xxx.*'

"Come alone!" Jane scoffed out loud. "This isn't a spy movie!" Jane looked at her hands—they were shaking. She felt a horrible premonition that the others were going to kill her. But she wondered about Jack still. He had said he had a plan and that she should trust him. So, perhaps there was hope. Perhaps that plan was meant to save her.

"So confusing," she said, shaking her head then looking at Death. "Don't be too certain that you're going to take me on a journey. I'm going to give them a few surprises if they try anything."

Jane checked her watch, she had five hours to prepare. "If they do try to kill me they'd better make sure I'm dead because I'm going to rip them all a new one if they don't."

She emptied her backpack out onto the bed then started to repack it with the items she thought she might need for a reckoning in the graveyard.

"Come alone. Ha!"

Chapter 29

I t was a quarter to eight o'clock when Jack turned the corner onto Church Road. The sun was low on the horizon and it dipped in and out of sight behind trees as Jack walked alongside the cottages. He spotted Ginny sat on the graveyard wall in a patch of bright sunlight. She was looking away from him, facing the sun with her chin lifted to savour the last of its warmth.

Jack wondered what terrors the night would hold and whether the plan he had cobbled together would work. He watched Ginny, wrapped in the warmth of the sun. A lot relied on Ginny's poison. He hoped she knew what she was doing because one small mistake could kill them all.

Jack stopped behind a tree trunk to be out of sight of Ginny then looked up and down the road for Dave but couldn't see him. He took a clear plastic bottle from the front pocket of his jeans, removed the lid and drank the rest of the water that it contained. Then he put the bottle back in his front pocket and pulled his T-shirt down so that it hung just over the top of the bottle, concealing it from view.

He tucked the bottle lid into his back pocket then walked around the tree and headed for Ginny.

So far so good, he thought. "Hi Ginny," he called out, to give her fair warning of his approach.

Ginny turned slowly, reluctant to look away from the reddening sun. "Hi Jack." She sounded relaxed and her gaze was level and unflustered. Her hair was tied-back, business-like. She held a backpack across her front that Jack assumed contained the poison.

"Any sign of Dave?" Jack asked.

"I think he's inside the church because the organ was playing earlier. It stopped five minutes ago, I guess. But I haven't been in to check... I felt a bit safer out here."

"Is the poison in the bag? Did you manage to get the dosage right?" Jack continued with his questions.

"Don't worry. I know what I'm doing. I've got the doses right, even though Death killed me again—the message was the same as before by the way, so I suppose that means if Death knows what we're doing then we must be doing the right thing. Otherwise the message would have been different, right? Or he would have tried to stop us by now. Of course, if Death doesn't know what we're doing then God only knows if we're doing the right thing. We'll find out afterwards I guess."

"Yeah maybe." Jack replied while thinking to himself that Ginny was still trying to justify their plan. "Do you think we're doing the right thing?"

"I'm here with a bag of poison, aren't I? Of course, I think this is the right thing to do. I'm just saying I don't know for sure that it's the right thing... and we won't know until it's done... once Jane is dead," she added.

"Don't say those words."

"Why not? It's what we're doing isn't it? Murdering Jane. I'm not calling it anything other than what it is."

"I'm trying not to think about what we're doing."

"Jack?"

"Yes."

"Say it."

"No."

"Say it Jack. Or, I don't believe that you want to do it. Say it so that you and I both know that you know what we are doing. Say it, or I'm walking away." Ginny went to move so Jack grabbed her shoulder. He stayed like that for a moment, his face twisting in a hidden battle. Then he sighed.

"Okay. I want to kill Jane."

"Are you sure Jack? Because I really want to know that you mean to kill Jane. That you're okay with this. That you think we should poison her—murder her."

"Yes! Alright. Yes, I think we should murder Jane. Just stop saying it..."

"Okay... it's the right thing to do."

"Oi, losers!" Dave's voice rang through the graveyard.

Jack let go of Ginny and turned to see Dave striding towards them from the church.

"Anyone having second thoughts?" Dave continued.

"No," Jack replied as Ginny shook her head.

Dave looked from one of them to the other. "Good, let's go behind the church where we can't be seen, and where we can hide the body."

"... the body?"

"Yeah, your soon to be dead girlfriend. That's what we're here to do isn't it? Kill your girlfriend?" Dave looked

172

hard at Jack—trying to see if he was having second thoughts. Probing for weakness, or any sign that Jack might have been planning on double-crossing him. "Well?" he challenged.

Jack realised that he was being tested. "Yes, I want to stop the nightmares. Yes, I want to sleep at night. Yes, I want Death to stop killing me. Yes, I think Death wants us to kill Jane. Yes! I want to kill Jane." He glared defiantly at Dave.

"Well okay then," Dave replied. "Let's go somewhere quiet that we can hide her body, so it doesn't get discovered for a while. Because then, if it doesn't get discovered for a while, it will decompose, and it will be harder for the police to determine how she died. So, let's go this way." Dave pointed.

They all looked at each other, waiting for someone else to take the lead. None of them wanted to be at the front in case someone was planning a double-cross. Maybe someone would be too tempted by an unprotected back and decide to just club the person in front to the ground. Their friendship, if it could be called that, unravelled.

"Ladies first," offered Dave with a smile.

"No thanks."

"I'll go first," said Jack, starting to not care, and worrying about his plan. He just wanted to get on with it now. For it all to be over and done with. And he worried about all the things that could go wrong. He glanced back as he walked, in case anyone decided to hit him from behind, but Dave was a healthy distance behind him, and Ginny an equally healthy distance behind Dave. They were all cautious of each other and respectful of the nervousness they each carried.

Jack pretended to study his surroundings as he looked left and right, trying to catch a glimpse of Dave in the corner of his eye. The low sun created long shadows in the graveyard causing the dark shapes of statues and gravestones to merge together into conjoined abominations on the ground. Winged gravestones, an angel with two heads, cherubs peering from behind trees, another angel hunched over as if old and broken. Jack walked through the disfigured shadows deeper into the graveyard and down to the weeping willows by the stream.

As he descended, the sun dropped behind a distant hill allowing shadow to banish light. Cool replaced warm on his cheek and a sense of foreboding settled uneasily on his shoulders. Jack stopped and looked back at Dave and Ginny.

"If we poison her under the willow it could be days before she's discovered," said Dave. "Or we poison her here and drag her under the willow. Either works for me. What do you think Jack? Here or the willow?" Dave asked, testing Jack's resolve again.

Jack checked his watch. "Jane will be here in ten minutes—we need to get on with it."

"That's the spirit!" Dave said in a deliberately cheery voice.

"Right," said Ginny as she arrived. She dropped to her knees and rummaged in her backpack.

"How did you get Jane to agree to come?" Dave asked, probing again for anything that might indicate that he was being setup.

"Easy," replied Jack

"Easy? She must be suspicious."

"No. I used something that neither of you two seem to have realised yet."

"Oh yes? What's that then?"

"I told Jane that Death doesn't kill us when we're together—only when we're alone. So, we were all going to hang out and drink some brandy shots at the graveyard, just to get some respite from Death. And that she should come as well. I sort of made it seem like we were all going anyway, and she would be the only one on her own if she didn't come too."

Dave looked surprised. "You're right. I hadn't noticed that—obvious as well. Nice one Jack." Dave nodded at Jack, acknowledging his well thought out observation.

"Okay," said Ginny standing up. She had three test-tubes with cork stoppers in the top of each one. A label was affixed to the side of each. "Dave, this is yours. Jack, this is yours. And, the last one is mine."

Dave looked at the tube he had been given. His name was written in neat handwriting on the label. "Wait, I was thinking I could choose which one I want to drink. Then I would know that you weren't giving me poison."

"It's not poison, it's antidote."

"Let me drink yours then."

"You can't." Ginny shook her head.

"No, this isn't right," Dave pressed. "Put them all together. I'll chose one, then Jack chooses one and you get the last one. That's the only way."

Ginny shook her head again. "I've measured the amount of antidote that we require according to our bodyweight. The amount we each need is different. I've measured it out to the milligram, and if we don't drink exactly the right amount we could die when we take the poison. Or, die from the antidote, it's not meant to be taken on its own. That's why I wrote the names on the side. You have to drink your one, not someone else's."

"No way, you could be poisoning me."

"Yes, I could but remember we decided that Death was telling us that Jane should be the one to die. So, why would I kill you?"

Dave wrestled with this. He looked to his right as if for inspiration amongst the branches of the willow trees. Ginny followed his eyes instinctively, and for a second both Dave and Ginny looked away from Jack.

Jack had been waiting for a moment just like this. His whole plan hinged on it. Quickly while the other two were turned away, he pulled at the cork on the test-tube, lifted his T-shirt an inch, and poured the contents of the test-tube into the bottle in his pocket. Then he closed his hand over the test-tube, hiding the contents, and lifted it up to his chin.

"Just get on with it," he said. Dave and Ginny looked back at him, so Jack put the tube to his lips—still shielding the empty contents—and tipped his head back. A last drop landed on his tongue, so he tasted the antidote as he pretended to swallow. "It tastes bitter." He smacked his lips. "Sorry to rush you but I need to meet Jane."

"Is she not meeting us here?" Dave was suspicious again.

"She won't walk in here on her own—we always meet outside. She'll be suspicious if we don't." Jack replied and handed Ginny the empty vial. "You can drink the antidote or not Dave, but I doubt we'll get Jane to drink the poison unless we all drink it."

Dave paused then pulled out the cork and drank the liquid down.

"Bottoms up," said Ginny and followed suit.

"Okay, I'll be back in a minute." Jack turned and walked away back up towards the church.

The graveyard was different already. The onset of dusk had quietened the birds in the trees. They rustled around hidden in the leaves, trying to find the best spots for roosting through the night. Jack avoided clumps of swarming midges as he wound his way through the gravestones. He had a lump in his throat. He was scared.

He stretched out his legs to speed up and walk off the fear, but also because he was eager to see Jane one last time. He clenched and unclenched his hands as he tried to stop the tremors that were silently building. His mind whispered to him. 'No Jack don't do it,' but he knew he had to. He knew this was the only way. He knew the only way to stop Death was with a death. They had been told that many times. It was fact. One of them must die.

Jack reached the low, stone wall that surrounded the graveyard and stepped over onto the path. He took a couple of deep breaths then looked around. No sign of Jane, or the Jane of Death. A car trundled down the road, so he stepped behind a tree to avoid being seen and it passed by without stopping. He felt secretive, furtive. He knew that what he was going to do was wrong. Guilt weighed down on him, trying to force him to change his mind. To find another way. But he came up blank. There was only one way and he was already on that path. The path that separated Jane and him forever. The path that ended their lives together in the most horrible way.

But, at least Jane's path will go on, he thought, as he caught sight of her down by the bridge. At least she will live. At least she will see the dawn at the end of this worst of nights. "I love you," he mouthed to her distant figure.

Chapter 30

O n the outskirts of Middle Gratestone, in a grassy field across which daisies and dandelions added speckles of yellow and white, a collection of creatures assembled. At their head, a boy dressed in a smart shirt and chinos, dirtied with grime and stained in patches, raised an arm in preparation of advancing his army into the town.

He was sat astride a giant spider, like a knight of old, his hands gripping the abundant brown hair that sprang from the spider's back. The spider he had chosen as his mount was exotic.

Orange hair grew from its head, interlaced with yellow and red hues that waved like meadow grass in the wind that blew down the valley. Two large eyes were mounted between two smaller eyes dead centre of the almost square head, and two more eyes mounted further back allowed the spider an almost 360-degree view of the world. The two large eyes were perfectly mirrored, and reflected the blue sky patched in puffs of white cloud, and the green grass speckled with yellow. The two smaller eyes, set next to the large eyes, copied the reflection of their larger companions. Beneath all four, hung black mandibles banded in yellow and bristling in long white hair. Mucus clung to the mandibles like hot wax to a candle. The mucus shivered as the mandibles twitched in anticipation of a forthcoming meal.

Alfred applied pressure to the spider's side with his left knee and turned the spider slowly on its yellow and black banded legs so that he could view his army.

Not all the people camping in the field had survived the transformation from human to spider. Deformed carcases—part human and part spider—were scattered around. Malformed with giant spider legs protruding from human backs, mandibles grown partway out of heads, and human torsos swollen into giant hair-covered abdomens fit to burst.

Evil had wrought destruction in this green field, but Alfred didn't care. He felt no loss—no pity. Because in front of him stood eight giant spiders. They were all different. Some compact and covered in hair, others great gangling things with tiny bodies and enormously long thin legs that spanned at least ten metres. Two spiders bore the white skull across their backs that Alfred's favourite spiders carried with pride. Another was jet black and had strong armoured legs and black red-rimmed eyes that reflected nothing of their surroundings.

There were signs of movement on the backs of some of the giant spiders. Rats nestled there, in the coarse hairs that patched the giant's bodies. Smaller normal-sized spiders also hitched a ride, webbing themselves onto their larger cousins.

Alfred completed his circle with the spider then dropped his arm and pointed forwards to the church spire visible in the distance. He didn't say anything—he didn't need to—his control of the creatures was now absolute. The crows lifted from the trees, cawing in excitement, their flat rasping cries sounding like the doors to hell creaking open. The hawk screeched overhead as it flew off, straight as an arrow towards the spire. And Alfred's army moved as one through the field, leaving behind collapsed tents and broken bodies as a portent to the coming destruction of Middle Gratestone.

They moved from the field and into the wood that separated the campsite from the old rectory field that bordered the church graveyard. The giant spiders flowed through the woods picking their way through the tangles between the trees. They moved across ditches, over mossy banks and through clearings covered in seas of bluebells. Alfred ducked down low and moulded himself onto the spider to avoid the low-hanging branches that tried to claw at him and rip him off the spider's back.

He urged his army on through the woods, impatient to be in the town already and start his war. For that's what this was—his war. For the first time in over one-hundred-years he had the initiative. He was doing what he wanted to do when he wanted to do it, and no one was going to stop him. He felt the power of his army surge through him. He was completely linked to them now; their fate was shared. They would fight together, they would kill together, and they would win together. His army sensed Alfred's certainty of the outcome of the upcoming battle. His certainty that they would obliterate their enemies and feast on their bodies. That victory would be theirs, and that today was the day that victory would be achieved. They surged forward—fighting through the wood.

Dusk was nearing as they emerged from the trees onto a narrow tarmac lane. There were no cars, just a couple of secluded cottages with narrow front gardens laid to grass and bordered with flowers. In one of the gardens, two girls sat on a trampoline sharing an iPad. Behind them, the two pretty cottages were mirrors of each other. Both had two-up, two-down windows, a red painted door set between the two downstairs windows and red-tiled roofs.

Into this beautiful setting strode Alfred's army. The spiders crashed through the high hedge that lined the wood and stepped out into the road while the crows swooped in and lined the apex of the cottage rooftops to better look down on the girls.

There was a pause, at least five to ten seconds while the girls processed what they could see. Was it real? Was it a trick? Were they dreaming? Were they in danger? Then one screamed—high pitched and piercing—it ripped through the spring evening, followed closely by the scream of the other girl. They both scrambled for the opening of the safety netting around the trampoline. The net was supposed to keep them from falling out, but now it ensnared them. They wriggled through at the same time, getting in each other's way then dropped to the ground together in a tangled heap of pink and yellow.

The cottage door burst open and a man rushed out to the girls. He thought they had fallen, and one was hurt but they leapt up from the ground and ran at him screaming. He could see the fear in their frantic movements, their flailing arms and their eyes that turned from him to look back at the lane. The man followed their gaze and took in the giant spiders lined up on the road. He saw the boy astride the spider in the centre of their ranks. His immediate thought was they must be mechanical or elaborate models. Perhaps they had wheels? Maybe they had been driven here or pushed? Maybe this was a hoax or a carnival?

Thoughts and ideas raced around his head, trying to distract him from the truth of what he could see. Experience told him they could not be real. His intellect told him that giant spiders didn't exist. But the animal instinct inside him recognised the predators in front of him and the real danger that they posed to the girls crowding around his legs. His heartrate rose and pumped his body full of adrenalin. His hands balled into fists and his mind raced as he worked through options in his brain, discarding them one after the other.

The spiders moved forward so the man backed up towards the door of the cottage. He reached for his pocket to retrieve his mobile phone, but it was on charge inside on the kitchen worktop.

The spider carrying the boy on its back crossed the wooden garden fence and stepped into the garden. The boy's expression drew the man's gaze. He wasn't smiling. He had murder in his narrowed eyes. Hate distorted his handsome features into something terrible that defied description. It was alien to the man, unworldly, and it shouldn't exist on the face of a boy. It shouldn't exist in the beautiful setting of an English countryside cottage. The expression was older than the boy. It was worn and had seen much. It raged at the innocent life that it desperately wanted to snuff out. The expression conveyed suffering, murder, revenge.

The man didn't try to talk to the boy. He could see talking was futile, so he quickly ushered the girls inside and locked the door behind him.

"Upstairs. Get upstairs," he shouted at the girls then rushed to close the downstairs windows and lock the backdoor before following the girls. He closed the upstairs windows as well then found the girls cowering together in one of the bedrooms. "It'll be okay," he comforted them and drew them together into a big hug. "Don't worry... we'll be safe here."

Chapter 31

Jane set off in good time to make the eight o'clock meeting... meet... whatever Jack had called it in his spy talk. "Come alone!" she scoffed out loud. "Ridiculous!"

She wondered what had led him to say such a thing. It wasn't like she had ever met Jack with her mum and dad in tow before so why would he think that now? It wasn't right or natural for him to think like that unless he had another motive, perhaps a dark motive. Or maybe he had just panicked and typed the first thing that came into his head. No, that wasn't like Jack though. He sometimes rewrote short one-sentence texts two or three times before sending them, so this email was most likely the same.

He knew she was more than likely to come alone anyway so why say come alone? Unless he wanted her to do the opposite! Perhaps he said don't bring someone because he wanted her to bring someone! Maybe for protection!

"No, that can't be it," Jane mumbled. If he wanted her to bring someone he would have just said so in the email. Jack wasn't... complicated. He would have just said—unless the email was for someone else as well. Perhaps he sent a blind copy to Dave and Ginny, so they could see that Jack had told her to come alone.

"You're overthinking this Jane," she scolded herself. No, Jack wanted her to come alone—pure and simple, and he just had to say so. He couldn't rely on her just coming alone without prompting her to do just that, even though it was blatantly obvious that was what she would have done anyway.

"Ridiculous," she scoffed again, then blew out her cheeks and looked up. She was nearly at the bottom of the lane. All she had to do was turn right into Church Road, cross the bridge and she would arrive at the church.

She stopped walking. It seemed too soon. Too soon to arrive at the church—too soon to meet Jack—too soon to die. Maybe she should turn back? Go home? Run? Hide? Her resolve started to fail. Then she remembered her hockey mantra—the words she said as part of her pre-match routine. The words that always steadied her and gave her strength.

"I will win," she said. "I will win," louder this time. "I will win," even louder. "Okay, let's go," she encouraged herself to walk again. Her breathing settled, and her strength returned. Jack will help me, she thought. Jack has a plan. I just need to trust him. She reached the corner and paused again. Last chance to turn back she thought, then strode forward and turned into Church Road.

The sun was below the high hedge that ran along the bottom part of Church Road. It flickered through twigs and branches disturbing Jane's vision as she walked. Light flashed in the corner of her eye like a tic, alternating between bright sunlight and cool shade. Jane squinted—trying to lessen the hypnotic effect and the queasy feeling it caused in her stomach.

It was too much. She stopped and looked away catching a glimpse of Death looming behind her. The flashing sun angered Jane, so she vented her frustration on the angel of death. "Is this what you do to everybody..." she snapped at Death, "...hang around like a wet fart? I bet you're great at parties. The life and soul yeah? Looming over the shoulder of your next victim. Maybe they die because you're there... not that you're there because they die. Have you thought about that? Perhaps it's your fault? Perhaps you're the cause?

"Yes you... your fault! You distract them. From driving their car... and that's why they crashed, or that's why they miss their footing and trip over. It's your fault. You cause it. How does that make you feel?"

Death remained motionless behind Jane, staring over her head as if watching someone in the distance—Jane resisted the temptation to turn and check.

"GO AWAY!" she screamed, but the angel of death remained impassive like a stone statue set in the tarmac of the road for cars to circle. Just stone, empty and lifeless, devoid of feeling. Except Jane knew she wasn't lifeless—she was something else—she was Death. And she was following Jane around as she always followed around all the soon-to-be-dead people of the world. She followed them, then once they were dead, carried their souls onto the next place. Now it was Jane's turn.

"Go away," Jane said again, but her voice was hushed this time. It carried no power or conviction. The black mist

187

in the angel of death's eyes swirled and moved like hot smoke. It was mesmerising and dangerous at the same time. It compelled Jane to move closer and further away in equal measure. It had the same hypnotic effect of fire drawing her in to its deadly embrace with the magic of its beauty but scaring her off at the same time with the threat of its hot flames. Jane shook her head and pulled her eyes away. "I hate you," she told Death. Then continued walking to what she thought was her own certain death. It had to be.

She crossed the bridge without stopping to look at the stream below. She could hear it gurgling and splashing through the arch of the bridge—calling her back to stare into its transparent depths. She ignored the sweet melody and walked slowly on as the sun dipped below the horizon, throwing a shroud of grey over the graveyard to her left. Only the high church remained lit by the sun, like a beacon over the growing dark below. Jane looked up at the tower, wishing she could fly up out of the shade into the sunlight above like the crows that were silently circling the church spire.

A shadow separated from one of the trees that lined the road then stepped into the path. Jane's eyes were drawn down from the tower towards the movement. She recognised the tall frame of Jack, though his features and expression were indistinct at this distance in the gloom.

Jane's breath caught in her throat. She couldn't see if Jack was smiling and suddenly that seemed very important. For a long second, she couldn't get air in or out of her lungs and her step faltered. She tried to squint and see Jack's face. She tried to breathe and force her lungs to start working. Then Jack's smile came into view and Jane regained control—her breath came back, and she sucked in the calming air and closed the distance between her and Jack.

She wondered if this was how walking to your own execution felt—to the hangman's noose, or the axeman's chopping block. She had always wondered how people could walk calmly to their own deaths. Why didn't they kick and scream? But now here she was, walking to her own execution—the condemned woman. Walking like a lemming towards the cliff edge, or a sheep to the slaughter house. Her feet shuffled forward of their own accord as her mind tried to work out how to escape, but Jack had her in his gaze—it was too late to escape.

"Hey," Jack said.

"Hi Jack," her voice wavered.

Jack walked the last steps between them and took Jane's hands. He looked worried. "Jane, we haven't got long—the others will get suspicious if we don't go down to them soon." He pulled gently on her hand then turned away towing Jane along with him. "Behind this tree," he instructed, then once out of view of the graveyard, he turned back to her. "Jane do you trust me?" The earnest tone startled her. Jack wasn't acting, he really needed to know the answer.

"Yes," the answer escaped before she even thought about the question.

189

"Jane, I need you to do something, and I need you to do it quickly without questioning why. Will you do that?"

"Do what?"

"That's the point Jane... don't ask me, just do it please... trust me."

"Jack I—"

"Will you do it?" Jack's voice was urgent. He was pleading.

She wanted to trust him. She wanted to believe that he meant her no harm. That he was trying to save her. But why the secrecy? She looked into his blue eyes. She could see truth and honesty there. She could see Jack—her beautiful honest Jack, and she decided that she had to believe in him. Nothing else mattered except that she must believe in Jack. Nothing else was more important. Not even her own life.

"Jane—"

"Yes... I trust you. I'll do it. Whatever it is."

"No questions—just do it?"

"No questions. I trust you Jack."

Jack visibly relaxed. The tension left his shoulders and his movements became fluid, like he had just been released from restraints. He reached into his pocket and pulled out an empty plastic bottle. "Drink this," he said to Jane.

Jane looked at the bottle again and saw there was a small amount of liquid swilling around in the bottom.

He thrust the bottle at her. "Drink it. Don't taste it, just drink and swallow it all."

She looked around the bottle swinging about in front of her face, into Jack's eyes. They were still honest, still beautiful. There were no lies to be seen there. She took the bottle and raised it to her lips while keeping her eyes fixed on Jack's eyes. She slowly tilted the bottle until she had to break eye contact then threw her head back and downed the liquid in one gulp. It was bitter, but she swallowed it down.

Jack took the bottle and pushed it back into his jeans pocket then pulled Jane in for an embrace. For a moment she kept her arms by her side, then she raised them and returned Jack's embrace, drawing him in and taking comfort from his strong presence.

"Is that a bottle in your pocket or are you just pleased to see me?"

"Hah!" Jack laughed and pulled back. "I love you Jane. I always have, and I always will."

Jane smiled in return. "Tell me that tomorrow," she said.

Jack looked sad for a moment then recovered. "Sure," he said but it was too late.

Jane's heart sank. He's poisoned me, she thought. He knows he won't be able to tell me he loves me tomorrow because he's poisoned me.

"Come on," said Jack. "We need to meet the others.

Jane let Jack pull her along by the hand. Normally she would never have trailed behind like a puppy dog on a leash, but she was scared. Scared she had made a mistake.

No, I trust him, she thought. It can't have been poison. Her feet moved numbly over the ground, the gravestones floating past like she was on a carousel. She could almost hear the fairground music in her head. Dead people lay under the gravestones, rotting away into the earth on which Jane walked. Soon the carousel ride would end, and she would join them underground—rotting, until the worms got her.

Her life didn't flash in front of her eyes, there was only gravestone after gravestone. She hadn't done anything with her life. She hadn't invented anything, saved anyone, helped anyone.

I've done nothing, she thought. And now I'm dead.

"Hey guys," Jack called out.

Jane looked up and saw Dave then Ginny. Come to gloat? Jane thought. Her voice spoke automatically. "Hi Ginny. Hi Dave," it said for her.

"Jane," Dave replied.

"Hi Jane," Ginny said. Then rushed up and hugged her. It was tight, fervent. Jane felt desperation in the hug. She returned it with equal force and clung on for a moment after Ginny released her. Ginny continued talking. "Come on let's go inside the willow. I've got a lantern that we can light the inside with, and drinks and snacks... it'll be creepy but cool."

"Yeah, we need some more creepy in our lives," Jane's automatic voice responded. She glanced back hoping that Death might have left her alone, but Death was still there,

192

behind her shoulder and apparently invisible to the other three.

"Are you expecting someone else?" asked Dave, seeing Jane looking over her shoulder. He peered into the growing gloom, still suspicious that he was going to be the victim of the murder tonight and not Jane.

Ginny reached the curtain of trailing branches that surrounded the willow tree and scooped a handful aside to form an entrance. "After you," she called out. The others filed in, followed lastly by Ginny. As she let go of the curtain, darkness fell in the interior of the willow.

Ginny pulled the lantern out of her bag and clicked the switch on the side. It was battery operated and burst into harsh LED light, so Ginny dimmed it down to a calming level and placed it on the ground. They all looked at each other then the four of them settled down around the lantern as if it were a campfire.

"Not bad Ginny," Jack complemented her.

"Well, I knew you boys wouldn't be organised. Anyone for a sausage roll?"

Dave coughed and cleared his throat. He had never been one to pass the opportunity to eat, even when the food was offered by Ginny. "Yep, why not," he coughed again.

"Count me in," said Jack.

"Maybe later," Jane declined with a shake of her head. Her stomach was knotted inside. All this small talk was making her even more nervous. Her stomach somersaulted as Ginny handed out the sausage rolls.

"So, shouldn't we wash it down with something?" suggested Dave, coughing between bites of the sausage roll. Then clearing his throat.

"Sure," said Ginny.

Jane looked more interested at the mention of drink. "What have you got?" she asked.

"I raided my dad's drinks cabinet at home. He certainly keeps it well stocked, I'll give him that. And hopefully he won't miss this little beauty!" Ginny produced a dark bottle with a flourish. "I have brandy."

"Yeeha," said Dave, in a rare show of glee.

"Okay, I've got some cups somewhere." Ginny rummaged in the backpack and produced some pink paper cups. "Sorry, they're the only cups I could find. They're left over from some distant birthday party I think."

"Don't worry, I just need a drink," Dave coughed again as Ginny passed him a cup.

"What shall we toast to?"

"Life?"

"Death?"

"What about both—cough," Dave managed.

"Okay," said Ginny as she poured a shot of brandy into each cup.

"To life and death," said Dave and downed the brandy in one gulp. Then broke into a coughing fit.

"Too strong for you Dave," asked Jack. "Life and death," he toasted and tossed the drink back making a great show of not being affected by the strong liquor.

194

"Life and death," Ginny added her toast to the others and took her drink down in two gulps, wincing between them. "Oh my God, that's strong."

Jane looked at the drink in her cup. It looked like black oil in the dim light of the lantern and just as unappetising. She wasn't a lover of alcohol at all and rarely partook in its consumption, unlike most teenagers in their small town. But today was a special day. She looked up at the other three all watching her expectantly. Her stomach twisted but she ignored it. Still she hesitated though. Was this the poison? No, it can't be—they've all just drunk some. There was no way that this could be a suicide pact. They were all too desperate to live; they didn't want to die.

"Life and death," she toasted and drank the fiery liquid down. It was sharp in her mouth and burned her throat on the way down then hit her already unsettled stomach. She joined Dave in coughing and clearing her throat. The two of them like a pair of old sailors coughing up forty years of nicotine. "Horrible," she gasped. The brandy seemed to be making it harder to breathe. She put her hand to her mouth and burped. "I feel awful," she managed.

"Well it's strong stuff," said Ginny and leant over to pat Jane on the back. "Come on Missus get a hold of yourself. That was the first of many!"

"Don't worry Jane... you'll be fine," said Jack.

"How do you know?" snapped Jane. The stress and the brandy were getting to her. If Jack had indeed poisoned her she needed to know, and she needed to know why before it was too late to find out. "How do you know I'll be fine? What makes you so sure?" she asked in a softer tone.

"Perhaps we should come clean now?" said Jack, looking at Ginny.

"Come clean?"

"Yes, tell Jane the truth.

"Oh yes, what truth is that Jack?" said Ginny.

"That you and Dave wanted to poison Jane of course," said Jack looking Ginny straight in the eye.

"Me and Dave! Hah! It's you and Dave that wanted to poison Jane not me. In fact, you came to me. You set this whole thing up. You're the instigator Jack. It was your idea to kill Jane—not mine. I don't know what you think you are doing telling Jane this now, but I know the truth Jack and it's too late for you to try and get some sick kind of forgiveness. Don't listen to him Jane. I'm your only friend here. I'm the one trying to save you from this pair of idiots."

"What! You want to kill Jane." Jack shouted.

"No Jack. No, I don't." Ginny shouted back over the lantern. Shadows filled the lines anger made on her face, turning them into cracks that writhed around as she shouted. "Jane is my friend. I've saved her life before and now I've saved it again."

"No, you haven't," retorted Jack. "You tried to poison her, but I've saved her. You'll get the victim you need alright, but it won't be Jane. Don't listen to her Jane she's lying. There's poison in that brandy, but Ginny gave me, Dave and her the antidote so that it won't kill us. But she wanted you to drink it and die Jane. Don't worry though, I tricked them both. I've given you my antidote, so you're going to be fine Jane. I've drunk the poison but not the antidote so I'm going to be the one to die, not you Jane. It's the only way I could save you. Otherwise these two murderers would have killed you. Well now it's over. Death will get the victim he needs, everything will be balanced again, and you can live your life Jane. I love you so much. I'm sorry we can't grow old together... I'm so sorry I won't get to marry you and live my life with you... but you'll get to live yours Jane."

Jane looked from Jack to Ginny. Jack looked triumphant. He was flushed and red-cheeked, but Ginny just stared at him open-mouthed in horror. Blood drained from her face, her mouth opened and closed then timidly she spoke. "Please tell me you did not give Jane the antidote."

"Yes, I gave her the antidote so your plan to kill her has failed!"

Jane watched Ginny and Jack stare at each other then without a word Dave slipped over sideways and vomited on the grass.

"Dave?" said Jack and jumped back. "Wait. What? He had the antidote. He should be fine."

"There is no antidote," said Ginny looking at Jane.

"No, you gave me and Dave the antidote earlier for the poison in the brandy."

"There is no poison in the brandy Jack. It's just brandy. The antidote was the poison—and you gave it to Jane."

"No!" said Jack in horror looking from Ginny to Jane.

Ginny nodded. "There's no such thing as an antidote you can take before taking poison Jack. It doesn't exist. God you're so gullible. The antidote was the poison Jack. I pretended it was the antidote to get you guys to drink it, and now you've given it Jane!" Ginny shouted out her frustration at Jack.

"Oh my God Jane!" Jack exclaimed as Jane fell back onto the grass. "Jane... oh my God... oh my God... Jane... Jane! I'm sorry I didn't know. I thought I was saving you— Ginny where's the antidote? Give it to her now."

"There is no antidote Jack. It's rat poison."

"Call an ambulance then. No, I'll call an ambulance." Jack pulled out his phone. "No signal—there's no signal!"

"You idiot Jack you gave Jane the poison thinking it was the antidote—you're such an idiot! You've ruined it all. You're so stupid."

"I'm stupid! What about you? You drank the poison as well, how's that for stupid?"

"Jack what are you not understanding? I didn't drink poison. The antidote I had was just water. You and Dave had the poison, and you gave yours to Jane. Dave drank his, Jane drank yours. That means only Jane and Dave were poisoned. Not me, and not you either. Just Dave and Jane. AND THERE IS NO ANTIDOTE!" Ginny screamed at Jack. "I thought you were betraying Jane—you, her

198

supposed boyfriend betraying her. So, I decided the only way to save Jane was to kill the two people that wanted her dead. That's you and Dave." Ginny clasped her hands to her head in exasperation.

Jack replied in a voice that had lost all its anger. His words ached with regret. They were hollow, emptied of hope and happiness and they bled into the air. "I wasn't betraying her—I was giving my life for her."

"Yes, I know that now—and between us both trying to save her, we've managed to kill her."

"Jack?" Jane's quiet voice cut through the interior of the willow tree. "Jack, how about we get up to the road and call that ambulance. I don't want to die here."

"Ugh," Dave groaned as he pushed himself up onto his knees then to his feet. He swayed unsteadily, hunched over supporting himself with his hands on his knees. "Unless one of you is going to hit me with something, I'm coming as well."

"Right," said Ginny, hoisting her bag on her shoulder but leaving the cups and brandy on the ground. "Let's go."

Jane watched Ginny step out through the curtain. Jack followed Ginny and gently pulled Jane with him. She looked back and glimpsed Dave vomiting again before she stepped through and let the willow branches sweep together behind her. Jane bumped into Jack though because he had stopped just outside the willow.

"Jack, keep moving," she encouraged. "I need to get to hospital. And, I need to get up that road while I can still walk."

Jack didn't reply but he pulled Jane out from behind him and clasped her tightly to his side. "Look up Jane," he said from over her bowed head.

"Ugh," Jane grunted then straightened herself with no small help from Jack's strong arm until she was stood upright, for what she felt might be the last time she could manage. Then she looked in absolute horror at the giant spiders in front of her. "Oh—I'm dead."

Chapter 32

Jane stared. It couldn't be real.

While she had remained within the dome of the willow tree's heavy foliage with Jack, Ginny and Dave, lit by the warm glow of Ginny's lantern, the graveyard had darkened to hues of grey. Now she was outside, she could see that within the grey, shadows and darkness shifted amongst the gravestones and statues. A black moving river of spiders, ebbed and flowed across the ground, rustling through blades of grass that bent under their combined weight of thousands then sprang back as they moved on. The spiders were restless. They flocked together like starlings on a summer evening, around the legs of the giant spiders that towered over them.

The giant spiders were arranged in a horseshoe formation around the willow—blocking the route back through the graveyard to Church Road. Rats moved around on the spiders, making it seem like the spider's bodies pulsated. And in the centre, astride a fearsome multi-coloured spider, sat Alfred. Like a king at the head of his army, he faced down his enemy.

"Jack, Ginny and Jane. My three favourite people all in one place. What a happy coincidence."

"Alfred, we need to get to the road. Jane's been poisoned and she needs to go to hospital," Jack said, seemingly unphased by Alfred's appearance and totally focused on getting Jane to a doctor.

"Poisoned! Well I hope she doesn't die before I kill her. That wouldn't be fair at all. I've waited a long time for this."

"Kill her! But why? What's she done to you?"

"I might ask you the same question Jack." Ginny said.

"I didn't mean to poison her Ginny, anyway it was your poison."

"You poisoned her!" laughed Alfred. "I thought you two loved each other. I know I've been away for a while but poisoning the love of your life! Something must have changed a lot around here because I remember you two as being sickeningly in love. This sounds all wrong to me... but at the same time, so right." Alfred tried to keep a stern face, but it dissolved into smiles and he laughed as he revelled in Jane's misfortune. "Tell me more," he instructed.

"Psst, keep him talking," Dave whispered from behind them. He was still within the confines of the willow and hadn't yet been seen by Alfred.

"It's a long story but okay," Jack said.

While Jack attempted to explain how Jane came to be poisoned, and Alfred listened with an amused smile and occasional laugh—Jane concentrated on Dave whispering to her from behind the curtain of willow branches.

"Psst, Jane, move back a step. Let me reach into your pack."

Jane realised what Dave wanted so she used a coughing fit to take a step backwards towards the willow. Alfred smirked at her coughing but didn't interrupt Jack who was still relating the story—with the occasional comment from

Ginny. Jane wasn't sure if Jack had heard Dave whispering, and was trying to buy them time, or if he was trying to justify his actions. Either way, Alfred was giving Jack his full attention.

She felt Dave's hands reach out and grab the zip on her backpack and slowly start to draw the zip down.

Please help us Dave, she thought to herself, willing Dave to save them all and not just himself. Surely it was in his best interests to do something that helped them all. Surely, he understood that if he and Jane were to survive the poisoning then they needed to work together against Alfred. She willed Dave to see her logic.

"—what? So you both tried to save her and ended up poisoning her! Alfred laughed again. A vindictive laugh that mocked Jack and Ginny's stupidity. "Who needs enemies when you have friends like you. My dad used to say that. I think I know what he meant now." Alfred continued to laugh so Jack and Ginny stayed quiet, drawing the moment out. "So, if I understand this correctly... Jane needs a hospital, or she will die?" he asked after his laughing had subsided.

"Yes," answered Jack.

"Well she deserves to die," spat Alfred, all trace of humour vanished in an instant. He glared pure hatred at the three teenagers in front of him. They were his enemies and he hated them, just like he hated their parents and grandparents. He hated their families, their heritage. He hated them all for what they had done to him and his own family one-hundred-years ago. Now it was time for revenge—to take life in return for the lives that had been taken—to steal in return for that which had been stolen. And then Alfred would be able to rest, to live his own life in peace as his parents should have done.

"I hate you!" he screamed. The giant spiders around him stirred, shifting their weight across their eight legs. They seemed to lean forward as if ready to pounce. "Your own stupidity is not going to stop my revenge. I'm going to kill you before you drop dead from the poison. You're not getting away from me that easily. This is my time. My revenge." Alfred's eyes blazed red, like before when he had freed himself from the statue in January. They were unworldly—supernatural—evil. Rage burned within him and erupted from his eyes in red flames.

"WAIT!" Jack screamed against Alfred's fury. "Wait, there's more you need to know."

But Alfred raised his arms in victory. He was losing himself to the rage. His sanity giving up to the insanity of the power that burned within him. The power that burned in hatred, stoked by rage, fanned by anger, fuelled by years of anguish.

"ALFRED, WE'VE SEEN DEATH!" Jack screamed, shielding his eyes with his hands to block out the red fire bursting from Alfred, and the wind that whipped around them. "He came to us... he's been killing us in our dreams. He wants one of us."

Somewhere. Somehow. Jack's words penetrated Alfred's conscious. The red fire withdrew in an instant, like a tap had been turned off. Jack lowered his hands and turned them palm up, offering peace.

"Death?" asked Alfred, out of breath, his chest heaving from the power he had displayed and the effort it had taken to regain control and then step back from the precipice from which he was about to leap.

"Yes, Alfred. Ever since you came back from the dead, Death has been visiting us. To start with it was just in our dreams, but lately it's been while we're awake as well. Like a daydream. Death kills us then tells us something. The same thing—every time.

"What? What does Death tell you?"

"That the balance is wrong, Alfred."

"What balance?" Alfred looked nervous now. He well remembered that he was only alive because of Death's generosity, and perhaps he knew better than all the others that Death's generosity could be reversed. He also knew of the power that Death commanded.

It was Death that had taken him from his body and held him captive in a statue for one-hundred-years. It was Death that had allowed his torture to go on day-after-day as he witnessed life move on without him. It was Death that had finally returned him to life—bitter and angry, corrupted forever by Death's false help. And it was Death that had taken his brother from him, his last surviving relative cruelly snatched away in front of him in what should have been his moment of glory. And in taking his brother at that point, Death had taken the last shred of hope that Alfred had. The last shred of humanity that he had clung to while imprisoned. Now he had only rage.

"What balance?" he repeated.

While Jack feigned thinking of the answer to Alfred's question, Dave put two aerosol bug bombs into Jane's hands. "I've taken off the lids, just press and throw when I say," he whispered. Then he sidestepped to get behind Ginny. Her hand was stretched behind her, opening and closing desperate to receive whatever weapon Dave gave her. Dave reached out and placed an aerosol can in her hand. "Same again, just press and throw," he said.

"The balance of life and death," answered Jack just before Alfred lost patience. "When Death brought you back to life he broke the rules. It wasn't something that he was supposed to do. You shouldn't be alive—bringing you back was wrong."

"MY DEATH WAS WRONG!" Alfred screamed at Jack, furious with him now.

"Yes Alfred, it was. I can't imagine what that was like for you, but—"

"Well now you won't have to imagine. Now you'll find out for yourself what dying feels like. My friends are going to bite you and poison you then feed on you until there is nothing left of you but bones. Your own mothers won't recognise you after the spiders and rats are finished."

"That won't help you, Alfred. Death has told us that you're the mistake," lied Jack. "He told us that the balance is wrong because you're alive."

"NOW!" shouted Dave as he burst from the willow.

Jane brought the two aerosol cans around to her front, pressed the button on top of each so that it locked open, then threw them into the midst of the spiders. She saw Ginny doing the same, and at the same time Dave threw a smoking bug bomb at the spider carrying Alfred on its back. Jane watched it leave a satisfying smoke trail in the air then spew smoke, laden with insecticide, from where it landed at the spider's feet. The giant spider recoiled, rearing backwards and spilling Alfred and some rats from its back as it did so.

The aerosol cans were also doing their job, spurting out insecticide gas that clouded the air around the willow. Jane watched Dave fiddling with a white canister that she recognised as the rape alarm that she carried in her backpack. He pulled a lanyard from the canister and the night was riven wide-open by the ear-splitting screech that erupted from the canister. Dave threw it in fright, trying to get the canister and the incredible noise it was emitting as far away from him as quickly as possible. It disappeared into the mist and smoke spewing from the bug bombs. The last image Jane had was of the giant spiders scattering into the night as Jack pulled her back into the confines of the willow.

Stomach cramps caused her to double over, then she retched, spewing into the dark that filled the inside of the willow. She was glad she couldn't see what she had vomited. Jack still had hold of her—she could just hear him shouting over the noise of the rape alarm. He pressed his mouth against her ear. "We need to get in the stream," he urged.

Jane nodded, and half pushed him, half hung on to him, as they made their way to the stream. She was vaguely aware of other shadows with them in the willow then the ground dropped away causing her to fall onto her knees in water. Jack hauled her up and dragged her out from the willow, out from the pitch-black into the half-light, then along the stream.

"Keep down," he urged. But Jane was already bent over, spewing again as Jack pulled her behind him. She felt a hand on her back. It was Ginny giving her a push, and behind Ginny came Dave, staggering gamely on.

They kept as low as they could to stay below the bank of the stream. The water came up to just above their knees, but cloying mud lay on the bottom, hampering their movement. Jane trusted in Jack to get her out of here, to get her to the road and onwards to hospital. There was nothing else she could do now. She felt her strength ebbing, her muscles spasming. Her vision came and went. Was it dark? How dark was it? Was she going blind? Was the poison making her blind? She started to panic. What if she went blind? She looked back at Dave. He was still with them, following on and spewing as he went. Dave took the poison first! she realised. So long as he is alive, I've got a chance. Keep going Jane, she said to herself. Just keep going.

The sound of the rape alarm faded as they put some distance between themselves and the willow.

Chapter 33

Adark fog swept across in front of Jane as her vision failed again. The fog moved like a shapeless wraith to wherever she turned her head, dancing and swaying over the surface of the stream and preventing her eyes from settling and focusing on anything of substance. Her breath rasped in her ears like a death rattle, each sounding like it was her last, as if every time she exhaled, her lungs were emptying for the last time and would never draw in air again. The poison was doing its work.

Her legs jerked, causing her to fall once more. The stream was deeper here, so despite putting her arms out in front of her to break her fall, she plunged under the water.

Jack hauled her up once again. "Come on," he urged, in a whisper. But Jane couldn't feel her legs and couldn't get them under her to stand. They flopped around beneath her like they were straw-filled and belonged to a string puppet.

Try as he might—Jack couldn't hold her upright to allow her to stand on her legs, so he picked her up and slung her over his shoulder in a fireman's lift.

Grunting with the effort of lifting her, he pressed on, up the stream and away from the willow. The mud sucked at his feet, causing him to stagger and lose his balance. He pushed himself back up, staggered a few more steps, then fell again.

While Jack struggled with Jane, and Dave just managed to keep up at the back, Ginny peeked over the edge of the bank into the graveyard. "We're not going to get away down the stream like this, and it's too far to the road from here."

"Well what else can we do?" Jack hissed as he shrugged Jane into a better position.

"Get on the church roof," replied Ginny. "Jane and I did it in reverse before... up through the tower then down the outside. But, I think we could climb the outbuildings and then scale the roof and into the tower. The church is right next to us. We can make it, then we call the police from there. We'll get reception on our phones from the tower and we might be able to defend ourselves better against the spiders from high ground."

Jack tried to think of something else but couldn't. And Ginny was right about the stream; they weren't going to get anywhere in the thick mud that lined the bottom. "Okay. Help me get Jane up the bank."

"Okay. I'll go first, you pass her up. Keep quiet though." As Ginny finished talking, the rape alarm warbled and fell silent. They all froze, feeling suddenly exposed by the silence. The graveyard came to life around them: rustling in the grass, rats squeaking, the scraping of hard carapace over stone—and a lone voice in the dark.

"I'll find you!" it shouted from back by the willow.

"Just go..." said Jane from Jack's back.

Jack moved to the bank and rolled Jane off his shoulder onto the grass then reached back and grabbed Dave's arm

211

and pulled him up. They all kept low, crawling in a line of four, with Ginny leading. She kept them straight, using the cover of the gravestones and statues to hide their progress towards the church.

"I'll find you! You can't hide from me. I've got eyes everywhere." Alfred shouted again from further away. And then a new sound—a police siren in the far distance. Was it coming because of them? Had someone reported a disturbance in the graveyard? Had they heard the rape alarm? Jane prayed quietly to herself that help was coming, as she crawled behind Ginny, with Jack behind her urging her on in a quiet, strong voice. Her Jack—her handsome Jack that had tried to save her but in fact had killed her—just like Death had said he would.

"We're nearly there. Keep going," whispered Ginny over her shoulder. She could see the white-washed side of the outbuilding just ahead. Against the wall were some water-butts and a large wooden picnic table with a bench seat attached to each of the long sides—somewhere for the vicar to take afternoon tea.

Ginny stood up and grabbed hold of one edge of the picnic table. "Jack, help me. Grab the other end and put the table against the wall."

Together they manoeuvred the table against the wall.

"Ginny, you go first, then I'll push Jane up. You'll have to grab her from the top and pull her up."

"Okay. Give me a bunk up then."

Jack stood on the table and put his back against the wall, he bent his knees and locked his hands together to provide a step for Ginny. She stepped into his hands and reached for the flat roof as Jack straightened his legs and pushed her up. Ginny's hands found the ledge and she pulled herself up with ease—standing on Jack's shoulders then his head.

"I'm up." Ginny turned and reached back down with an outstretched hand.

"Jane. You're next," she instructed.

Jane looked up from the ground. She was on her hands and knees still. Her legs and arms shook just with the effort of holding herself up. Her hands remained planted in the grass as if they had grown long roots that held them there, try as she might she couldn't lift them. The table might as well have been Mount Everest; Jane had no strength left to climb up to Jack—let alone the outbuilding to Ginny.

"Jane—" Dave slurred. "Go on."

"I can't—" was all she could muster as a sentence. Then Jack's strong hands took hold of her and once again lifted her onto his shoulder then onto the table. Jack steadied her on her feet in front of him then leant back against the wall.

"Step into my hands Jane," he said. "Please! You can do it."

Jane still couldn't feel her legs, or properly focus on Jack's hands. There was just a dark shade where Jack's hands must be. She swayed precariously on the table, then half stepped, half fell, into Jack's hands, and with the last of her strength pushed down on Jack and reached up for Ginny.

Ginny grabbed her wrists and hauled her up.

"THERE!" Alfred screamed from across the graveyard, spotting Ginny and Jane atop the roof.

"What's left in your backpack Jane?" Ginny asked, but Jane just wheezed in reply, struggling to breathe as the poison slowly prevented her blood from carrying oxygen around her body. So, Ginny, after getting no response, rolled Jane onto her front to access the backpack. Jane heard the zip open and felt Ginny's hands rummaging inside. Then Jack's voice. Jack? Where was he?

"Jack—" she mumbled.

"Come on Jack," Ginny shouted down and looked over the edge to see Jack lifting Dave onto the table. A rat jumped up using the bench to reach the table top. Jack grabbed it and flung it into the distance before it could do any harm. He jumped onto the table, next to Dave then kicked off another rat that had climbed up a table leg.

Dave leant against the wall, like Jack had done earlier. "You next," he said.

"No, you won't be able to get up."

"Neither will you mate."

"I'm not leaving you."

"Yes, you are Jack. I'm done for. I can't even stand anymore, and there is zero chance of you being able to lift me up that wall, but I just might be able to lift you... there's no sense in us both dying. Try to save Jane, you're her only hope now. She's the best of us Jack... the only one who stayed true to all of us. She should live—save her Jack. Go." Dave nodded with his head up the wall. "Rat!" he pointed, as another one reached the table top. Jack kicked it away, as Ginny threw down another smoking bug bomb in front of the table that spewed stinking, poisonous smoke into the air.

"The giant spiders are coming," she shouted down. "Get up here!"

"Go Jack. Go now before it's too late," Dave told him. "I'm sorry for everything Jack. Tell Jane that. Tell her I said sorry. I just got mad with you all. Go! Save Jane."

Jack nodded. "Thank you," he said, then stepped into Dave's hands and reached up. Dave hoisted Jack with the last of his strength then slumped against the wall and curled into a ball—waiting for the rats and spiders to come.

Chapter 34

Jack reached the flat-roofed top of the outbuilding and surveyed their position. The roof was about twenty feet long and ten feet deep. It looked and felt sturdy enough underfoot, so he hoped it would hold their weight. The front and two sides of the outbuilding both dropped about ten feet straight down to the ground, so aside from the picnic table that he and Ginny had placed against the wall, there was nothing for the creatures to use to climb up.

Behind them, the outbuilding adjoined the church at the bottom of the steeply sloping church roof. Although the slate rooftiles looked mossy and slippery, Jack thought they could find enough hand and footholds to climb the church roof to its apex. Or, they could traverse along to the large square church tower and climb that instead. Either option would get them high enough to get a phone signal then they could call for help. Jack quickly checked his phone but as he had suspected, the church roof was obscuring the signal—they needed more height.

He looked back. Ginny was busy spraying Jane and herself with copious amounts of insect repellent.

She saw Jack look over. "Close your eyes," she instructed, pointing the aerosol at Jack, and without waiting for Jack to reply, sprayed him all over.

Jack coughed. "That stuff stinks."

"Well let's hope the spiders think so as well," Ginny answered.

Jack moved over to Jane and rolled her onto her back while Ginny patrolled the edge of the roof. Jane's breathing was light and rapid as if she wasn't getting any air at all and she was unconscious. "Jane," Jack checked for a response, but she was oblivious to his presence. He grabbed hold of her under the arms and lifted her upper body off the roof then dragged her over to the bottom of the church roof and away from where the spiders would most likely attack.

"How's Dave?" he asked as he shuffled backwards.

Ginny peered over the edge, down into the shadows and smoke below. The rising of the full moon over the church roof behind them had relit the graveyard. The moon's silvery light illuminated the faces of the gravestones while white angel statues glowed with a corporeal luminescence that gave them life. The giant spiders were scattered around the graveyard but were now all heading in the direction of the church.

Directly below Ginny's vantage point, the ground was shaded from the moonlight and still shrouded in smoke from the gently hissing bug bombs that she had thrown down.

"Dave?" she called down into the darkness, but there was no answer. "I can't see him," she shouted over her shoulder.

"Okay, keep looking." Jack replied.

Ginny snorted back at him. She would decide what she was going to do next—not Jack. She kept an eye on the approaching giant spiders while rummaging through Jane's backpack. Inside, she found one remaining bug bomb, a pepper spray and a headtorch. She strapped the headtorch on then debated with herself whether to throw the other bug bomb.

Meanwhile, Jack had laid Jane back onto the church roof, so that she was in a half-sitting position. He examined her for a moment, checking her pulse and breathing then pulling his phone out to use the torch to light up her face. "Oh no!" he gasped. "Jane!"

Her skin was ash white and her lips blue. Her breath came in shallow gulps so far apart that after each breath Jack thought she had stopped breathing, then she spasmed and gulped a tiny breath again. It was as if every breath was her last and the wait between was excruciating.

"She needs a hospital," he called over to Ginny. "I've still got no signal though."

"We need to go up the roof then," Ginny threw the last bug bomb down into the graveyard then moved to help Jack. "Take an arm each and let's pull her up the roof together."

They positioned themselves on either side of Jane then started to pull her up. Each took a step, grabbed a handhold with their freehand and then hauled. The slate roof was steep, and their feet slipped, but they hauled Jane up one-foot at a time. Jack couldn't tell if Jane was breathing and they couldn't risk stopping to check—her head lolled from side-to-side, bumping over the rooftiles as they pulled her up. Slates dislodged under their feet but the gaps they left provided hand and footholds.

It was hard work, both Ginny and Jack grunted with the effort. They were only a third of the way up when a large black leg came over the edge of the outbuilding, scrabbling to gain purchase.

"They're coming!" Ginny yelled, as another black leg reached over the edge and pulled the spider slowly into view.

"It's too far to the top, we won't make it in time," said Jack, looking from the spider climbing onto the outbuilding below, to the church roof up above. "Ginny, you go. Run to the top and phone for help. Get the police here. Get the ambulance here. Phone everyone!"

Ginny nodded then let go of Jane and headed up the roof. She knew this was the only way. She had already figured it out. Then she remembered the pepper spray. "Jack, take this." She rolled the can down to him then carried on up the roof without looking back.

Progress was slower for Jack now. He could only manage to haul Jane one or two inches at a time, but he carried on anyway, edging himself up then bracing on the roof and hauling Jane after him. Inch-by-inch he kept moving. Below him, the first giant spider mounted the outbuilding then moved onto the church roof to start scrabbling its way up to Jack and Jane.

Jack rolled his upper body on top of Jane to hold her in place and shield her from the spider then he readied the pepper spray. As the spider closed in, rats dropped from its body and scurried straight up the roof towards Jane who was lying unconscious and helpless. Jack kicked away the first rat then squirted the remainder with a wide sweep of the pepper spray. The rats squeaked in pain and dispersed, leaving the spider alone.

It was a fearsome creature. Its eyes reflected the moon, turning them into white orbs that shone like car headlights, hypnotically dazzling Jack. The mandibles below the eyes, twitched together then apart like a crab's claw, flicking off great globs of mucus that splattered across the roof. Its first barbed leg reached Jane's foot, so Jack let loose with the pepper spray—squirting it into the spider's eyes and the gaping maw of a mouth behind the mandibles. It froze then reared backwards, turning completely over on to its back and rolling down the roof in a clawed ball. It hissed and writhed on the outbuilding then dropped away to the ground.

Jack sprayed a line of pepper spray below him to keep the rats away if they returned then carried on hauling Jane. He looked up, Ginny was astride the apex of the roof, speaking into her phone. He could just hear snatches of words but nothing tangible that he could make out as a meaningful sentence.

He looked backwards as another giant spider crested onto the outbuilding. Jack realised his progress up the roof was too slow, so he started to haul Jane on a diagonal, up and along the roof. Trying to gain distance from the spider by contouring away from the outbuilding towards the church tower.

The spider seemed to pause as if deciding whether to go after Ginny atop the roof or Jack and Jane up and along. Then, decision made, it headed up and along towards the juicier target of two prey rather than one.

As Jack cleared the line of the outbuilding, the drop to the ground opened beneath him. Now if he slipped down the church roof, he and Jane would plunge all the way to the ground below. The fall would at best leave them injured and at the mercy of Alfred and his spiders, but at worst it could perhaps even kill them. Jack started to think he had made a mistake, but it was too late to change his mind, so he continued to desperately haul Jane up and along.

The spider crossed from the outbuilding to the church roof then skirted along the bottom edge of the roof until it was directly below them—perhaps so it could ensnare them if Jack slipped.

"This is it!" Jack exclaimed. "Hold on Jane. GINNY!" he screamed.

Ginny looked down and saw Jack's plight. "They're coming. The police are coming, just hold on!"

"I know I've got to hold on," he replied under his breath. He looked back down. The spider took a step forward, so Jack readied the pepper spray. As he did, a crow flew out of the darkness into Jack's face and stabbed at his eyes. Jack dodged the sharp beak so that it raked his cheek. He grabbed at the bird as its wings beat at his face and its claws scratched at his skin drawing blood. It saw Jack's hands and reacted quickly, stabbing the back of his hand that held the pepper spray causing Jack to drop the can.

Then the crow was gone and once again its black feathers were cloaked by the darkness of night. The pepper spray rolled down the roof and dropped over the edge.

"Now!" Alfred's voice shouted in triumph from below. Jack could see him—sat astride a giant spider in the graveyard directing the creatures in their attack.

"Leave us alone!" Jack shouted down at Alfred.

"Never!" Alfred shouted back, bouncing around and laughing on the back of the spider.

Jack pushed up with his feet and hauled Jane with him. He only manged to move her an inch at most. The giant spider though, moved quickly up the roof to them. Its barbed legs had no trouble hooking into gaps in the roof and the rough edges of tiles. It reached them in seconds, so Jack again threw himself over Jane. "No!" Jack screamed—angry, frustrated and terrified all at the same time.

The spider reared over them. Its huge mass blocking out the view of the night sky, but instead of striking down with its poisonous fangs and filling them with poison, it stabbed down with a sharp barbed leg into Jane's ankle, hooking onto her trouser leg. Jane didn't flinch.

The spider stepped back, pulling Jane towards it, then edged back again, pulling Jane further down the roof towards the drop below.

Jack gripped Jane then braced with his legs, but the spider was strong and had the advantage of pulling downhill. Slate rooftiles gave way under Jack's feet and slid down the roof to fall and smash on the ground. The spider moved inexorably closer to the edge of the roof. Jack strained against it, his muscles burning—his will refusing to yield. He fought for every inch—for every fraction of an inch, but the spider was unstoppable, untiring—it showed no sign of strain. Jack could not win. He knew that, but he hung on anyway.

"I've got you," he whispered into Jane's ear. "I'll never let you go."

Jane gasped and choked then let out a long sigh.

Something was torn away from Jack—from inside him—from his soul, something that he should have carried with him forever. Something important, something precious, something he should have protected. Despair washed over him, like a light had just gone out and left him in darkness. He was alone. Jane had passed. She was gone.

Jack sobbed in anguish. It was a sound he had never made before. It sounded like someone else, not him. It hurt as it forced its way out and was followed by another and another. But he held on to Jane. The spider would not have her. Alfred would not have her.

He screamed at the spider. He locked his legs and leant backwards, pulling Jane up an inch, gaining ground from the spider for the first time. Then he stepped and pulled again. The spider's legs slid on the slates. It had strength but not enough grip on the unstable, slippery roof. Jane's trouser leg ripped and came away at the bottom, causing Jack to fall backwards, pulling Jane on top of him. He stood up quickly though and pulled Jane again, gaining valuable distance up the roof. The spider teetered at the edge of the roof—unbalanced, ready to fall over, but then one of its front legs gained a foothold and it hauled itself back up.

It rushed up the roof and stabbed Jane in the thigh with a barbed leg. The barbs hooked onto Jane's jeans and her flesh then the spider hauled back again. Jack lost purchase with his feet and he and Jane were pulled down to the edge. Still he refused to let go.

Again, he locked out his legs and leant back to strain against the spider. He clenched his teeth so hard his jaw muscles protruded.

"No!" he cried out through his teeth as once again the rooftiles gave way and he slipped towards the open drop.

The spider reached the edge and slowly moved off the roof, down the wall, allowing gravity to help it even more. It paused with four legs still on the roof and four scrabbling around on the wall searching for footholds. The fight with the boy was won now, it knew that for fact. It would drop down the wall and pull the girl over and the boy would fall with her. Once on the ground it would cocoon the girl while its brothers and sisters paralysed the boy then cocooned him as well. That was what its master wanted—so that was what it would do.

Jack knew that he had lost. He knew that now the spider had reached the wall that he wouldn't be able to haul Jane back up onto the roof. But he wouldn't let go. He would go over the edge with Jane. He wouldn't let her fall to the ground on her own and be at the mercy of the spiders and rats below. He would fall with her and break her fall with his own body then he would fight for her. He knew she was dead, but he would fight for her as if she was alive.

He hung on while the spider tried to negotiate the tricky roof edge without falling or losing its grip on Jane. Then Ginny appeared at his side. Jack looked up. She was stood next to him with her hands raised over her head holding a large slate rooftile. She launched it at the spider, using her height advantage due to the slope of the roof, and her furious aggression to propel the tile at speed.

The tile hit the spider hard, straight in one of its smaller eyes at the edge of the bank of four. It landed with a solid, satisfying crunch. As the tile dropped away it revealed a ruined eye—no longer black and spherical like the three eyes next to it. Green ooze spurted out from the crushed mess that remained.

The spider recoiled in pain causing it to lose grip on the roof with one of its front legs. Now only two legs held onto the roof supporting its weight, plus the one holding Jane. Jack and Ginny looked up, as once again, the sound of police sirens came from across the town.

"They're nearly here!" Ginny shouted out as she pulled at another rooftile, trying to wrench it out.

225

"Jane's dead." Jack panted, his strength almost spent.

"What? No..." Ginny looked at Jane, seeing her stillness for the first time. She stopped pulling at the tile and placed a hand on Jane's neck, trying to find a pulse. She turned the headtorch on and gently pulled back one of Jane's eyelids. Jane's eyes remained unresponsive—wide-open, staring but not seeing. "You're right Jack, she's gone. Let her go."

"No."

"We can escape to the tower Jack then get into the church... we'll be safe there. We can wait it out, let the police deal."

"No! I'm not leaving Jane. I'm not!"

The sirens were close now. Ginny looked between the safety of the tower and Jack's tug-of-war with the spider, then down at Alfred and the other spiders waiting in the graveyard.

"Let her go!" Alfred shouted up from below, clearly enjoying the spectacle.

Ginny felt her aggression rise. She wouldn't be cowed by anyone. She was Ginny Petherbridge. Her father was the mayor. This was her town. And it was time to fight back.

"Hold on Jack," she said, turning to prise out the tile she had been working at earlier.

"You can't win," shouted Alfred from the graveyard. "I'm going to—"

BOOM! Alfred's words were cut off by a deafening bang from the graveyard below. A bright flash accompanied the noise, lighting up the graveyard for a split-second, exposing

Alfred and his creatures in harsh white light as if lightning had struck. Alfred screamed in pain, and the spider on which he was mounted, staggered as if struck by a blow.

"I see you Alfred. I see you and I'm going to kill you!" A woman shouted out from the darkness. Then another huge boom sounded out from the dark, again illuminating the graveyard.

Jack and Ginny saw fire spurt from a shotgun held by a large woman covered in bloody bandages. Alfred screamed in pain again. "Get her! Get her now," he shouted at his army. All his creatures, except the wounded spider on which he sat and the one holding Jane, rushed at the woman. She broke the shotgun in the middle and pulled out the spent cartridges, then pushed in two new cartridges taken from a bag around her waist.

The giant spiders rushed towards her, but she was quicker. She got the shotgun to her shoulder and again it spat fire. Then the rats and the spiders reached her, and she disappeared in the melee of legs and claws. The shotgun boomed again from within the brawl, but this time the flash was contained by the mass of bodies.

Alfred clutched at his chest. Blood oozed from under his hands, from his head and neck and from his side, turning his clothes crimson red. The spider under him collapsed, throwing him to the floor. He picked himself up and staggered towards the church—focused on Ginny, Jack and Jane.

"Give her to me," he spat, dropping to one knee and wiping blood from his eyes. His power was waning as blood flowed from his wounds. He could sense he was mortally wounded by the shotgun blast. That this would be his last battle. He focused his efforts on controlling one spider—the one that fought against Jack and Ginny for Jane's body.

"No! Never," shouted Jack—equally locked into the fight. Unrelenting, unyielding—he would not give up on Jane. Not ever.

Chapter 35

Jane's sight darkened, and her world went black. She tried to see Jack's face one last time, to look into his blue eyes and say goodbye. But she couldn't. She screamed out in frustration but made no sound. Her mind had detached from her body and she was trapped in darkness—unable to see, hear or feel anything. Her heart fluttered, trying to find a rhythm but the poison had done its work. Her heart beat one last time then stopped. She was dead.

She cast around in the darkness, trying to find something—anything, to help her find her way. She was cold and she was alone—adrift in a black ocean of nothing. She was as lost as a mariner at sea swallowed by waves, or a miner trapped underground by rocks after a cave-in. She was alone and in the dark with only her thoughts for company.

She pictured Jack in her mind—smiling at her, his blue eyes twinkling. His strong arms holding her. His laugh. His kindness. The way he looked at her.

Her thoughts diminished the darkness. She felt light reach out to her. She could see its glow in the distance. Its warmth and its comfort. She stretched towards it, trying to touch it with her fingertips. It was just beyond her, tantalisingly close. She willed it to take her, to lift her out of the darkness. She accepted it. She welcomed it. She let it in. At last she felt substance, and something took her hand.

Something tangible and solid. It grasped her hand and pulled her out of the dark and into the light.

As she left the dark, part of her fell away to remain behind. A part that she didn't need anymore. She was hauled to her feet. Light surrounded her, so she could see again. She was holding Death's hand. Death had hauled her out of the dark. It was her Death, her angel of death, and it stood before her clad in battle scarred armour holding Jane's hand in its scaled claws.

Jane looked down. Next to her, Jack and Ginny held onto her body. They heaved and strained against the spider that held her leg. Below them, Alfred knelt in the graveyard, blood dripping from him. He was white-faced and grim.

Jane released her hand from Death's grip. "Am I dead?" she asked.

"Your body is dead." Death answered her in a lady's voice, old but well-spoken. The voice was neither kind nor unkind. It was neutral and instead of invading Jane's thoughts like before, the words came from Death. "You cannot go back to it. You must move on," she continued.

"Move on to where?"

Death pondered before answering, running a black tongue over her pointed teeth as she thought. Smoke swirled in her eyes, and her long hair and cloak flowed out behind her as if she was stood in a fierce wind. Jane could not feel any gusts at all, but they snatched at Death, cracking her cloak like a flag in a gale.

"You have a choice to make." Death replied. "I have chosen you. Now you must decide if you will answer my call."

"You've chosen me for what?"

"I can no longer continue in my role as a guide to those who require passage. I have been the reaper of life for millennia, but I have broken the covenant by which I am bound. The balance must be restored. A life for a life. It is my life that is forfeit. My life will restore the balance. I must go into the light then a new covenant can be made, and the balance restored. You will take my place. You will become the bearer of souls. You will make a new covenant and lead all those that leave this world into the light. This is how it must be."

"You want me to become you? Why? Why me?"

"I have chosen you."

"But why?"

"Because you are neither pure nor un-pure, good nor evil. You are equally perfect and imperfect, you are corrupted and incorruptible. You will not judge a soul when it is confused. You will take it to the light as the covenant requires and in doing so life and death will continue. You will perpetuate the balance that my passing will restore. This we must do, or life will cease. I have chosen you."

"What if I don't want to do it?"

"I have chosen you."

"But if I don't want to do it..."

"Look at your friends. Their lives hang in the balance. They will be pulled from the roof and perish on the ground below."

Jane looked. Jack's legs were scrabbling at the very edge of the roof and Ginny was holding onto him while the spider moved steadily over the edge, pulling them both with it.

Death continued talking. "Alfred's body is dying. It can no longer support life. His death is inevitable, but will you take him to the light before or after your friends fall to their death. That can be your decision to make if you take my place."

Jane looked from Death, to her friends teetering on the edge of the roof, then back at Death. She knew she had to decide right away. Jack and Ginny were out of time.

"Is it worth it? Is being you worth giving up going into the light?"

"I have never been into the light—I do not know what is there. But I know that being the Grim Reaper as I am often called, is not always grim. It is both good and bad. People will fear you. They will fear your arrival and be scared when they see you, but once they are accepting of their death they will be grateful for your aid in their passing. So yes, I would say, it is worth it."

"Okay!" Jane snapped at Death, seeing Jack starting to overbalance at the roof edge. "Yes, I'll do it. But how?"

Death sighed in gratitude. "Thank you, Jane."

"You're welcome," she replied, just wanting to get on with it now that her mind was made up.

Death pulled her sword from its scabbard, and for the second time, offered it to Jane hilt first. "Take my sword and strike me down."

"What?"

"A life for a life Jane—the balance must be restored. Now, strike me down."

"No!"

"Strike me down. Cleave my breast and pierce my heart. You must do this."

"No. I'm not strong enough. You've got armour on."

"You have the strength Jane. You need only take the sword. Then you will feel your strength. Take it and strike me down."

Jane panicked. She had no time, she had no strength— she couldn't do this! She grabbed the offered sword and pulled it away. Her arms automatically lifted the sword up into an attack stance from which she could strike. Strength flooded her like electricity charging her muscles. She felt powerful, mighty, undefeatable—she was a warrior, a soldier. She had purpose and the strength and means to fulfil that purpose.

Death nodded. "Thank you," she said.

Jane swung the sword with all her might. It sliced through the battle-scarred breast plate, cut through the angel of death's heart and emerged out the other side—completely cleaving Death in two. The space where Death had been, turned to black as if a shadow was all that remained. Death's armour, scabbard and all her vestments fell to the floor. The shadow blew away into the night.

A lady dressed in a simple white linen dress appeared in Death's place. She was beautiful. "Go now," she said. "I will wait here."

Jane knew what she had to do. The knowledge of all time and creation filled her. She thought to go to Alfred—then she was there. She had not walked or run—she had just thought to go and instantaneously she was at Alfred's side.

Without hesitation she reached inside him and pulled his soul from his body. It came willingly—and it was beautiful and pure, but then there was a resistance. Something tried to pull back, to wrest the soul from Jane and drag it back into Alfred's body. Jane pulled harder and with a rip another part of Alfred left his body. It was black and seething—it was the malice and ill-will that had been poured into Alfred by others—his torturers and murderers, all the miscreants and thieves that had done him wrong. The black seething mass was now as much a part of Alfred as his pure soul. The two joined together—merging into one being.

"No!" Alfred screamed, thrashing and raging against Jane.

From the corner of her eye she saw the giant spider that had been fighting Jack and Ginny for control of her body release its grip and drop away to the ground. It turned left and right in confusion then scuttled away into the dark. Jack and Ginny held onto each other on the roof edge gasping for air. They were safe.

"No!" Alfred continued to rage at Jane—powerless in her grasp. She let go. He stood still, quiet now he had been released, and looked at his body, lying bloodied on the ground. "Put me back," he demanded.

"No."

"Put me back!"

"Your body is dead. I can't put you back."

"PUT ME BACK!"

"So that you can kill my friends? So that you can kill others? No, I will not put you back. Your body is dead, it's time for you to move on Alfred."

Alfred's demeanour changed, his shoulders slumped. "But it isn't fair. What was done to me was wrong."

"Yes, Alfred it was. But the people that hurt you, they're not here. They died and moved on a long time ago. There is nothing you can do to hurt them back."

"Yes, there is." Alfred's defiance came back. "I can kill their families like they killed mine. I can cut off their poisonous bloodlines and stop their infection from spreading. I'll be doing a good thing ridding the world of their filth. They killed my family, so I can kill theirs. I want my revenge."

Jane paused to take a moment to think. She could see all of Alfred's life laid out behind him, the events that had led to his first death. How he had been saved with good intention by Death and how his mind had broken while he waited to live again. Jane could see and feel all the real pain that Alfred had endured and how it had changed him. The pain boiled within him.

"Alfred you must let go of the pain of your past. Let me take you onwards to the light—there you can find the peace and happiness that you want, that you deserve.

"I don't want to go."

"That's your choice, Alfred."

"What? My choice?"

"Yes, of course. I cannot force you to go to the light, I can only show you the way."

"What if I don't go?"

"Then you will be lost. You will stay here alone and confused. You will become ever more frustrated and angry until you forget who you are and forget why you never went into the light. Then you will ask me to take you because you won't know what else to do."

Alfred started to walk away from Jane, fading as he went. The further he got from her the more transparent he became, like a photograph fading in the sun. His voice became distant. "I'm not going to the light. I'm staying here."

"You will be lost."

"I'm not—" Alfred faded to nothing.

Jane sighed. She looked to the roof. Jack and Ginny appeared frozen in time as if her conversation with Alfred had occurred in an instant. Jane realised that this was how she would have sufficient time to get around the world to provide safe passage to those that had passed. She existed outside of time.

She thought to go to the roof then she was there. The lady in the white linen dress still waited.

"I'm ready to go now," she said and smiled at Jane. "I've waited a very long time. Thank you, Jane."

Jane nodded. She wasn't quite sure what to say. She had a one-hundred percent failure rate of getting people to pass so far. She looked at Jack and Ginny, still frozen in time, holding onto Jane's body.

"Goodbye Jack," she whispered, her eyes tearing.

Something nagged at her. A sense that she hadn't had before. It was as clear as sight, as loud as hearing. She felt it as keenly as ice on her skin. It was a sense of death—newly acquired. It was vivid and bright in her mind. She could feel death nearby—the lady in the bandages, Mildred. She needed guiding to the light. And a little further away a man and two girls in a cottage, one girl his daughter the other her friend, Robert, Isabel and Anna. They had died in terror and agony, and they too needed guiding to the light. Jane shuddered and prayed that she was equal to the task.

Printed in Great Britain
by Amazon